H-2

Enjoy

Carol Szcremers

The Look Alike

CAROL FRANCISCO

authorHOUSE®

AuthorHouse™
1663 Liberty Drive
Bloomington, IN 47403
www.authorhouse.com
Phone: 1 (800) 839-8640

Published by AuthorHouse 03/24/2017

ISBN: 978-1-5246-8488-4 (sc)
ISBN: 978-1-5246-8486-0 (hc)
ISBN: 978-1-5246-8487-7 (e)

Library of Congress Control Number: 2017904458

Print information available on the last page.

Any people depicted in stock imagery provided by Thinkstock are models, and such images are being used for illustrative purposes only.
Certain stock imagery © Thinkstock.

This book is printed on acid-free paper.

ACKNOWLEDGEMENT

First and foremost for the love of my family, my husband John, daughter and her family Stephine & Kenny, and my four grandchildren: Sierra, Koy, Zach, and Eli.

To my friend Amy Houser-Gunsallus for her steadfast belief in me, all the encouragement and the setting of deadlines.

To Gypsy Tree Photography {Amy Cutler} creating the photo for the cover and taking my picture.

For my editor Kelly Thomas, all your help was invaluable, and thank you for the excitement you brought to this project...

Contents

CHAPTER 1

ETHAN CANTRELL AND CRAIG STIEN sat at the best steakhouse in town, Sam's Place, finally able to enjoy a leisurely lunch. The last six weeks had consisted of either a quick sandwich break or takeout. It was great to be able to sit and enjoy the smell of steaks cooking.

They sat talking about the Hudson merger. "I'm glad we got that merger under our belts," Ethan said. "Big brother had his hands full with it."

Craig stretched and replied, "He sure did. I don't know anyone else who could have pulled it off. Rhys can do anything he sets out to do." Both men looked up to Rhys; he was more than just a big brother, he was a role model to them.

After finishing up their lunch, they decided to linger over another cup of coffee. It felt good just enjoying the strong, bitter taste.

Ethan looked around to see who else might have stopped in, and a woman on the other side of the room caught his eye. For a moment, he was disoriented by her appearance. He couldn't believe whether what he was seeing was real or not. Was he really seeing who he thought he was seeing? Glancing away and pinching his eyes shut, he determined that it couldn't be *her*. Ethan had to take another look.

Focusing on the corner table again, his deep voice showed evidence of anger when he spoke. "Damn, I don't believe it."

Craig could hear the anger in his voice. Looking up, he encountered it in Ethan's eyes also. Craig had no idea as to why or what had altered Ethan's mood to such a degree. "What is it?"

Silently taking a few deep breaths, the new tension undeniably in the air, Ethan indicated the source of his ire with a tilt of his head. Craig looked across the room to the corner table. He didn't see anything out of place or different. What would cause this kind of reaction in his friend?

"Well?" Ethan asked with a touch of impatience.

Craig did not see what he should be seeing, so he shook his head and shrugged.

Ethan didn't understand why his friend was so calm about this. He feared his anger was about to surface, and not in a good way. Taking a few deep breaths to calm himself, he looked to the far side of the room. In a low voice, he said, "You need to look over at the table in the far corner there, and then tell me you don't see her or understand why I'm so angry."

Craig, still unsure of what had caused Ethan's outburst, started scanning all the tables around the area Ethan had indicated. At the far table sat a woman, but Craig couldn't really see her. When she finally turned to the waiter though, her full face was revealed to the two men.

Suddenly, he knew what had caused Ethan's reaction. "Do you really think it could be her?"

For Ethan, there was no doubt. He was sure. Disgusted, he said, "Do you doubt it?" Needing no answer, he went on. "What do you think we should do?"

Considering the best course of action, Craig asked, "Do you think one of us should stay and keep an eye on her, just in case she leaves? Do you think we should just call Rhys, and tell him to come down here to meet us?"

For the first time in many years, Ethan was feeling unsure how to handle a problem. He wasn't looking forward to telling his brother the news. He needed to think over the possibilities. This kind of information needed to be told face to face, not over a phone. It's not that his brother wouldn't believe him, but as there had been so many false sightings of this woman over the years, Ethan didn't want to take a chance. He took his phone out and snapped a picture, knowing it wouldn't be very good but would help in the telling of his story.

Considering she had just arrived for lunch, and the place was extra busy today, Ethan decided they had at least an hour to talk with Rhys and get back here before she left.

The decision made, he turned to Craig. "No. We'll both go back to the office. I want Rhys to know we're serious, that it's not another mistake. Both of us have seen her, right? The picture should confirm it enough, and I know he will want to take some kind of action right away. Just think—he spent the last five years of his life searching for the bitch. Having the cops think he did away with her and not letting up on him? And there *she* sits across the room from us, looking like she doesn't have a care in the world. Who would have thought we would find her after all these years, and right under our noses?"

It was time for them to leave. They stood and threw money on the table for their lunch. Ethan turned for one last look, just to be positive it really was her. Shaking his head, he said, "Let's get to the office. I'm not looking forward to this, but there's no time to waste—and it's time for this to be taken care of once and for all. Rhys needs to deal with her and finish this business. Then maybe he will be able to find a future for himself and get on with living."

Both of them knew they would be seeing fireworks shortly. Ethan wondered about how many casualties would be counted before it was all over and what the fallout would show—or if any of them would come out of this whole.

Ethan also wondered if they should notify Matt Landon. He decided that Rhys would decide when, and if, Matt should be told.

Chapter 2

Skylar Evans sat in Sam's Place, considering what course her life should take at this time. Interrupted from her thoughts, and looking up at the waiter, she spoke. "Excuse me?" The waiter paused by her table to see what she wanted. "Could you bring me the newspaper to look at?"

The waiter nodded and left, only to return a minute later with the paper. "Are you about ready to order yet, miss?"

"Yes, I'll have the steak salad with French dressing, some garlic bread, and a diet soda, please." After writing up the order, the waiter turned and left.

Skylar just sat there and relished the moment. She finally had that feeling of being free, something she hadn't felt for a very long time. After nearly eleven years of taking care of others, she was now able to finally come and go as she wanted. It sure was a different feeling.

For a change, everything was going her way. She was going to start living her life to the fullest and please herself for a while.

Her lunch had arrived, but she hardly tasted it. She was eating, but Skylar's mind was on things in the past. She began thinking back on her life, wanting to remember why she had chosen to start over in this state and this town. Maybe thinking on it would help her to put everything behind her. She had decided to relegate it to the past where it finally belonged – it was all the way back in 2005 – but she had to think on it first. It wasn't easy to just let everything go.

★★★

Skylar's grandmother, Jane, had been living a full and active life in her own home in Maple Grove, Pennsylvania. Jane had decided to walk the

4

short distance to the local store to pick up a couple of things and walked into a robbery in progress. She was shot and pistol-whipped by one of the robbers. This caused her to have a stroke, and she was left almost completely paralyzed as a result. She needed constant care when she got out of the hospital. Jane couldn't live by herself anymore.

So the decision was made that Granny Jane would come home to live with Skylar and her family. Mother began to take care of all of Jane's needs, and this caused her father to be put into the background. He didn't care for this at all and began getting angry at everything. He began drinking a lot and not coming home in the evenings.

Skylar had never really gotten along with her father, and as she grew older, he seemed to resent her more and more. There were times that she had even thought that she saw hate in his eyes, but she convinced herself that it couldn't be true. She couldn't understand why he felt this way; after all, Skylar was only a young girl at the time.

On her twelfth birthday, her father was just *gone*. He told his wife, Lainey, that he couldn't take it anymore, and he just walked out. It was bad enough, he felt, that he had to share his wife's attention with the child, but when Jane came to live with them, he'd had enough. He was tired of all of the competition for Lainey's time.

Skylar had overheard this conversation and was devastated to learn her father didn't like to share her mother. That was the day that Lainey changed toward Jane and Skylar. She became a bitter, cold woman who blamed others for her husband's defection. Years later, Skylar would know the reasons for many of the things that had already occurred, as well as those that were yet to come.

After her father left, there was a shortage of money. Lainey had to find work to keep the household going. They couldn't afford to have someone come in to take care of Granny Jane during the day while Skylar was at school, so her mother took a job at night. Lainey took care of Jane during the day, and Skylar watched her while her mother was at work.

Lainey told Skylar, "Since I take care of Granny Jane during the day, it's only fair if you take care of her in the evenings. After all, if we could afford it, we would just put her in a home."

Jane was a huge burden to her only daughter. Lainey hated her mother, and the burden Jane caused, just made Lainey resent her only daughter even more. She blamed them for all her problems. If not for those two, she would have a husband and wouldn't have to work all the time. Lainey never let Skylar and Jane forget that it was because of them that George had left. This had resulted in their loss of income and caused Lainey to go to work.

When Skylar began taking care of her grandmother, she was never allowed to linger after school to hang out with the other kids. She always had to come straight home and begin taking care of her grandmother. Lainey said this was so Skylar could feed Jane and give her mother some time to get ready for work.

High School became harder on Skylar; so many changes were going on in her life, and she didn't understand. It would have been so much easier if Granny Jane could talk and maybe explain some of the changes to her. She wanted to have friends and hang out just like everyone else, but at that time, her mother said there were to be no dates or outside activities, since she had enough to do at home. Lainey said outside distraction would take away from Skylar's responsibilities, and she had better not forget that those responsibilities were her own fault.

It was hard to believe that this all started back when Skylar turned twelve, a hard time in a young girl's life.

Skylar wondered how many years would she live like this. Was she never to be allowed to have friends, or find out what life was really all about? This couldn't be all there was to it. At seventeen, she had nothing to speak of. Life seemed like it was just passing by as she watched the others in her class have fun and go places.

One early spring, Granny Jane passed away and an enormous burden was lifted from Skylar's shoulders. She hadn't wanted her to die, but she was at peace now. It was time now for Skylar to think about her future. Could she be a normal, carefree, teenage girl with friends? Just maybe she could go out on a date, or to one of the school ballgames. And there were the school dances to consider – her junior prom was in a couple of weeks.

But Lainey had other ideas for her daughter. She told Skylar there wasn't enough money coming in again. Since Jane's disability check wasn't coming any longer to help pay the bills, Skylar would have to look for a job to help out.

One of Skylar's teachers helped her to get a job. She was going to go to work as a girl-Friday to the secretaries of Mr. Harry Blackwell.

Skylar, nor her mother, realized that this new job would be a new beginning for Skylar.

Skylar caught on very quickly to her duties at the office. Working became an escape from home. Filing, answering phones, delivering mail to all the departments, and then having others ask her opinion on things, began to give Skylar some confidence in herself. The secretaries all helped her and she began thinking of them as family. Time seemed to fly when she was at work. The secretaries passed on how well Skylar was doing. Her work began to impress Mr. Blackwell, and she found herself with more and more to do, and even more responsibilities. Skylar began helping Mrs. Blackwell with things on Saturdays, which caused some trouble with her mother at first, until Lainey found out that Skylar was getting paid extra for that.

The Blackwells decided to hire someone to find out everything they could about Skylar. When they received the report, they were shocked by how much she had dealt with in her young life thus far. They had never guessed that she was the product of a broken home and a mother who bordered on abusive. Harry and his wife decided they wanted to change things for her; they felt she was the sweetest girl around. They had never been able to have children, so they had a lot of love to give, and they wanted to give it to Skylar.

Skylar likewise grew to love the Blackwells. They began to do things for Skylar, spending time with her and having her come to their house for dinner a couple of times a week. They always said it was work-related so as not to get Skylar into trouble with her mother. The three of them became like a family, and the Blackwells felt as though Skylar was the daughter they never had.

When Skylar's senior year was half over, she decided nothing was keeping her from the prom this year, even if she went by herself. She shared this desire with the Blackwells, and they felt the same, wanting Skylar to have some good memories from high school.

Skylar received a pay raise at this time, too. She decided to withhold this information from her mother. So without Lainey being aware of it, Skylar began a checking account with her extra money. When the time came for her night out, she would be ready for almost anything that would come up.

Since the Blackwells knew all about what Skylar's life had been like up until this point, they would often ask her to come and live with them. She always thanked them for their kindness, but said she couldn't leave her mother all alone. As much as she would have liked to do just that, as she loved them as family, she could never forget the responsibilities her mother had placed on her for so many years. She could not leave her mother.

It was now the week before the prom, and Skylar had already picked out her dress and had paid for it over the last few months. It wasn't the prettiest or the most expensive, but it was hers, that's what mattered most of all.

The Blackwells had plans of helping prom night be a night to remember for the rest of her life. It was going to be a paid holiday, that way Lainey couldn't say anything about it. Then, they would call her into their office to give Skylar the gown that they had specially made for her. They couldn't wait to see her face. She had had so little in her life, they felt she deserved to have something special.

Seniors were given prom day off, and it was time to go and pick up all the extras. Just about to go out on her errands, the phone rang. It was the office calling. Skylar was wanted in the boss's office as soon as possible. On her way across town, Skylar began wondering what could be wrong. Was one of the Blackwells sick? Had someone called off, and they needed her to fill in?

After Skylar made her way into the office, Jean Blackwell nodded her head and said, "Sit down child."

Taking a chair, Skylar began to be frightened. Seeing this reaction on her face, Harry tried to reassure her about why she was there. "It's not what you're probably thinking. It's nothing bad at all. In fact, I hope it makes your day, and evening, all the brighter."

Finally, Jean walked over and reached down behind her husband's desk to draw out a large dress box. Skylar was so surprised that she choked up, and was almost crying. Upon opening the box, Skylar found a dress beyond her wildest dreams – it had to be the most beautiful gown ever created. The color was aqua-green, with sequins that made it look like diamonds. The gown was also strapless, and it made her think of a fairy princess. Looking up at these two people, Skylar had a lump in her throat the size of a golf ball.

Jean reached to take Skylar's hand and said, "I know you are probably going to tell us you can't accept this, but don't do it. Please let us do this for you. We know you already picked out a dress, but it was your second choice and we want you to have your first choice. You have come to mean almost everything to Harry and me, so don't cheat us out of the chance to spoil you like you should have been spoiled all these years."

Harry handed her an envelope and added in a fatherly tone, "This is money for any accessories that you might need. We also have a car for you to use."

Skylar couldn't believe all this; it was like being Cinderella, and having a fairy Godmother. But in this case, it was Godparents. How had she gotten so lucky to have these people in her life at this time? Skylar had often wished that they had really been her parents, but then felt incredibly guilty. It was unfair to feel that way when she had a real mother. That alone made her better off than some others in this world.

Jean had to clear her throat before she could speak. "Don't just stand around here child, get going. And we want you to have the time of your life tonight." The Blackwells hugged Skylar, then gave her a gentle push toward the door.

Her feet barely touched the ground the whole afternoon. Going from store to store, and being able to buy everything she thought she would need to make her dream night come true made her feel mature and independent for the first time in her life.

When she reached home, Skylar ran up the stairs with so much excitement, ready to shout about how happy she was. She couldn't wait to share all this with her mother, about everything that had happened on this day. Finding her mother in the kitchen, Skylar was about to speak when Lainey slapped her and began screaming at her and waving an envelope around.

Skylar was at a loss, and hurt, and couldn't understand why her mother was behaving as she was. Then, with a sickening feeling, Skylar was finally able to understand what was being said. "You little bitch! You had the nerve to open a checking account and then hide it from me? And then to have a dress delivered here? Well, let me show you what I think of your dress." Skylar was frightened by the look in her mother's eyes. Lainey took a knife and began slicing the dress into shreds, unleashing the anger that was running rampant within her mind.

Lainey continued screaming, "How dare you even consider taking time off work to go to a stupid dance? Just who the hell do you think you are, anyway?" She was grabbing at Skylar again by this time and started shaking her.

Skylar couldn't believe how her mother was acting. Why was she this angry? Pulling away, she looked at her mother through the tears in her own eyes. "I wish it had been you instead of my Granny Jane that had died. I never thought about hating anyone like this before, but I think I could really hate you," Skylar spat.

Turning away, Skylar ran from the house and jumped into the car. Locking the doors, she put her head on the steering wheel and sobbed. Why, oh why, was her mother like that? After starting the car, she began driving around aimlessly. What should she do? Where should she go now?

Then she remembered, the Blackwells would be there for her, and she was still going to the prom. So with this thought in her mind, Skylar turned around and headed to Harry and Jean's home. Once again, the love of the Blackwells would get her through, and she would take them up on their offer of living with them finally.

Little did Skylar know, her life was not going to be the way she thought. This wasn't going to be an easy fix.

After arriving at the Blackwell's home and running up to the door, Skylar fell into Jean's arms, sobbing out the story with little control over her emotions. Jean listened and then said, "Let's get all your stuff out of the car and get you ready for this prom of yours, and I want to take some pictures, so there better be a giant smile in the near future."

After getting ready and having many pictures taken, Skylar was ready to go, but there was another surprise waiting for her. Harry cleared his throat. "Well, how about you allowing an old man another wish? Why don't you use our limo and driver for the night? And when you get home, you can sleep in the room we told you that you could have whenever you wanted it. We will help you sort out everything else tomorrow, so don't worry tonight. Remember, we love you, and have a great time."

When Skylar arrived at the school, quite a few people were very surprised she was attending as she had never seemed to want to join in with anything before. There was hardly one dance that wasn't asked for as some of the boys had been crushing on Skylar for the last few years. Right around midnight, the police came for Skylar, telling her about her mother's accident. A neighbor had been out walking when she saw Skylar leave. Apparently, her mother had run out into the road screaming her name, and was struck down by a hit-an-run driver. The police officers said they would help her get to the hospital. They helped her into the car, then proceeded to the hospital as they tried to explain again what had taken place. Skylar asked them to call the Blackwells for her so they would know she wasn't going back to their home.

The officers were very kind, waiting until the Blackwells arrived before leaving. It seemed like forever before the doctor came out to see her. On the way home, Skylar began thinking over what Dr. Jones had told her. Lainey's spine had been injured severely; there was no operation to help her at this time. Her mother would be an invalid the rest of her life. He talked about nursing facilities and other things about constant care.

So it was to begin all over again, and what would she do this time? Harry and Jean said they could all live in their home and they would hire someone to help so Skylar would be able to have a life other than what she had had before. But Skylar had told them no, it was up to her to take care of her mother in her own home. She wouldn't have them being miserable due to her mother being there, and her mother would be hateful and not thank them for their kindnesses. After all, Skylar felt deep inside that it was all her fault for saying the things she did to her mom.

It took several years, but when Lainey finally passed away, the Blackwells were there to support Skylar and help with all that needed to be done. After the funeral, they found many things that needed to be gone through. Harry and Jean began going through Lainey's personal papers to help out with the financial side of things.

Skylar found that Lainey had told her many lies, especially when it came to the facts about her father. It was found that George Evans wasn't really her father. Skylar now knew why he had disliked her to the point of hate. Instead, Skylar found that she had no idea who her father could be. Was it a one-night stand, or did Lainey know who had made her pregnant?

While going through the last of Lainey's things, Skylar picked up the Bible that her mother had always kept on her nightstand. This was something she had never let Skylar touch. Leafing through it, she soon discovered why this had been. There was a picture, and it took Skylar's breath away. In it was a man – he could be no one but her real father as the resemblance was uncanny – and beside him, was a young version of Skylar's mother. Looking back at the man, she tried checking off all the features they shared. It seemed she was a softer version. There was the same nose and chin, the eyes – what could she say?

Was it any wonder Lainey had guarded this so dearly? It was probably the reason George had hated both Lainey and Skyler so much. To have a picture of this man around would be bad enough, but to have his child around would be so much worse – a constant reminder to George of Lainey's past.

As Skylar looked at the picture, she could see that the two people pictured seemed deeply in love. It was written in their eyes for all the world to see. What had happened to the man in the picture? Had he died, or was it something else that tore the couple apart?

Jean came across some other papers while cleaning the other bedroom. They had been between the mattress and box springs, hidden. Taking them out to the other two, she handed them to Skylar to read. These secret papers had to do with Granny Jane – she had left a large insurance policy in Skylar's name. As Skylar was a minor at the time, Lainey assumed control, or so she thought.

Jane had made provisions just in case. If the child was not of age when she died, the money would be placed into a trust until Skylar reached the age of twenty-five. This left Lainey with only paperwork to deal with, which it didn't seem she kept up on.

Had she resented her daughter so much to keep this from her? After rereading it, Skylar found out that she could have drawn on the money if it was necessary. Things could have been so much easier for them both if Lainey had only told her about it. If she would have taken Skylar to the bank, she would have been able to get Skylar to sign over a part of it to her, as this provision had been written into the trust. Did Lainey never read the trust documents thoroughly, or did she just not want Skylar to have anything extra? Skylar would have done it to help out if she had only known about it. In the end, Lainey had only hurt herself.

A few weeks later, Skylar decided to sale everything. She was going to give up her job, and start a new life in a different place. So with the decision made, she went over to see Harry and Jean one more time to ask for help.

She made all of the arrangements – placed the house with a good realtor, cleaned everything out, even donated what she didn't need. It was time for her to tell Harry about giving a four-week notice. To let him know it was time for her to go out into the big old world and explore. She knew there were others at work who could take over for her.

Harry couldn't believe what Skylar was contemplating; he knew she couldn't live in *that* house any longer due to the past. But to move away from everyone else who loved her, namely Jean and himself? He implored, "You aren't seriously going to just give up on everything and leave? You are one of the best personal assistants in the business now! Besides, you are like a daughter to us. I know you have turned down many offers from others to stay here, but I thought, now with your mother gone, you would just take a little time. Everyone you know lives in this town and there are only strangers out there.

"You know you are like a daughter to Jean and myself. It's hard to let go when it seems we have only had you for a few years. I don't want to let you leave us alone again. We love you."

With tears threatening, Skylar tried to explain why. "At twenty-five, I think it's long overdue for me to leave the nest. It's time for me to have a life just for myself, and see what is out there in the world.

"I need to know that I can make it on my own, without all the help. I love you both more than my next breath, but let me try this. Don't use emotional blackmail on me to stay. Just let go for a little while. We will still talk on the phone. Who knows, I might not like it out there, and want to come running back home to the two of you, where I know it's safe."

Knowing they would have to accept the inevitable, or lose Skylar altogether, both sighed with acceptance and tears in their eyes.

Harry wanted to make sure if she wasn't staying here to work with him, he would make certain whoever she did go to work for would appreciate the kind of prize they were getting. So with that thought he said, "As much as it pains me, I will give you a letter of recommendation and some names of other companies that would like to have you."

Jean was crying when she said, "Remember you can always come back. If not to work here in our company, at least to Harry and myself. You know you have become my daughter in my heart – I couldn't love you more if I would have given birth to you. All we want is for you to be happy in your life at last. It's harder to let go than I ever would have imagined. Our love will always be with you wherever you may be. And be sure I will be calling and checking that you are taking care of yourself."

This came straight from their hearts; they would miss each other more than any of them would ever realize.

★★★

So here she sat, at age twenty-five, picking at the remainder of her lunch and thinking over her past. Maybe another cup of coffee was what she needed. After thinking on all of this, her nerves were a little frayed. Maybe she should call Jean and talk with her, just to hear her voice again today.

Why had she thrown it all up in the air to come to this place? Just what had drawn her to this town, or for that matter, this state? She had asked herself this question more than once.

Yesterday she found the perfect apartment, and then signed a six-month lease with the Superintendent. It was fully furnished, so would save a lot of her time, and money, though that wasn't really an issue. Finding a bank close to her new home was a bonus also, so the transferring of her accounts was taken care of already. Some people would think she was reasonably well off, with the trust and the sale of the house. But she didn't think of herself that way.

Skylar didn't want to live off of this money. She was used to making her way in this world and wasn't about to sit around being idle. So with this thought in mind, she picked up the paper and decided it was time to see about a job.

CHAPTER 3

MEANWHILE, ACROSS TOWN, RHYS CANTRELL was sitting in his office listening to the story Ethan and Craig were telling him.

He couldn't, or more like it, *didn't* want to believe what he was hearing. After all this time, was it really going to come to an end? Could his quest be almost over? It was just too much to take in. His desk was starting to feel confining, so he got up and started to pace. All of a sudden, Rhys turned and shouted. "Are you absolutely positive about this? You couldn't be mistaken?" Rubbing his face, he took a deep breath. "Tell me again what happened."

Looking up at his brother, Ethan told him everything that had happened, and then he remembered about snapping the photo with his phone, so got it out to show his brother.

Rhys had stopped pacing and was staring out the window; he needed to think, but knew there wasn't much time to wait. Turning, he looked over at the two men. They both seemed so sure it was her. The picture wasn't really clear, due to the quality of the camera phone that took it, but it was making him consider that this could be his missing wife. Running his hand through his hair, he sighed. He really couldn't take a chance. He had to go and see for himself, find out if it was her, and where she had been all this time.

Rhys buzzed for his secretary, and in a tone that broke no argument, he said. "Just listen, and say nothing until I'm finished. Call my father into the office and have him handle anything that's urgent. Also, tell him I'll let him know what's going on later.

"The department heads should be able to handle anything pertaining to them, and if not, refer them to my father. Clear my calendar, keep track of anything of a personal nature, and I'll be out of the office until further notice. Understood?"

"Yes, Mr. Cantrell. I'll take care of everything immediately," Mrs. Straw answered.

Grabbing his jacket while shutting off the intercom, he turned to the others and then headed to the door. "Let's go."

Riding over to Sam's Place, the car was in total silence. This gave Rhys time to think on things further, and to feel a whole range of things. First, there had been the passion with them, and the happiness, and then the anger at her subsequent betrayal, and finally the pain and disillusionment.

Soon enough, though, Rhys's thoughts, thankfully, turned to the present. He needed to draw on the old numbness he felt back then; he couldn't let his emotions run wild and get the better of him. Because if he did, he knew his actions wouldn't be what he would want in the end. He needed to think this through. What would be the best course of action to take?

Ethan and Craig had all been there with Rhys when their unhappiness had started, all the way to the final result of her disappearance. And then, even further, to the police thinking he had done something to her. They knew the hell that Rhys had lived through for the last five years. The agony of having no way to correct the situation or knowing what the situation really was.

Now it was only a matter of minutes before everything would be blowing sky-high. Ethan knew his brother was feeling a great deal of rage at this point, and he hoped Rhys would be able to control himself when he finally saw the woman in the coffee shop.

While pulling up in front of the restaurant, Rhys inquired as to her whereabouts inside. "Just where was she sitting when you were here? I want you both to stay in the car."

"She was on the left as you're going in, at the far corner," Craig told Rhys.

Rhys nodded in confirmation and found his way inside the small shop. He decided he would get a cup of coffee, and was told it would be a few minutes as they were brewing a fresh pot. He took his time looking around, but it was like his gaze had been irresistibly drawn to her. He saw her right away. Shaking his head, not really wanting to believe it was her, because for five years, he had wondered where she was, and then, all of a sudden, she was right there in front of him. To be able to see her again, so suddenly, was overwhelming.

Bree Anna, he sighed to himself. There his wife sat across the room from him, just reading the damn paper. It was unreal – but they were right, it really was her. His control was almost to the limit again; he needed to cool off. He had to get out of there before he did something he would regret. Seeing the coffee he ordered was ready, he took it, and then walked outside. When he reached the sidewalk, he pitched the coffee into the trash with as much force as he dared to show. Taking a few deep breaths, he started to calm himself down.

What should he do next? Then, looking back towards the restaurant, a plan began to form in his mind. Would he be able to pull it off? Would it work out to his satisfaction? *Oh yes.* He knew now, with his mind's eye, it would indeed work. It just *had* to work or his sanity might be lost.

Walking back over to the car, Rhys saw the two men about to ask questions, and so he held up his hand to keep them quiet. Now was not the time to get into any discussions.

With a sly grin beginning on his face, Rhys said, "Start the car little brother, and be ready to drive. When I get in, head out toward the airport for starters. I'm thinking on taking her back to Grandfather's ranch. It should be interesting, of that I'm sure.

"Don't be surprised by my actions. Just be ready to go. I don't want to draw attention to ourselves by sticking around." Backing away from the car, Rhys went over to lean on the side of the building. He knew that the shade would conceal his presence while he was waiting for her. She wasn't going to disappear this time. No sir, *that* was not going to happen.

CHAPTER 4

SKYLAR HAD ONLY CIRCLED TWO of the ads in the paper. One was for personal assistant and the other was for administrative assistant, both with bigger companies. She would call and arrange interviews and then call Harry and tell him about both and see what he thought. If neither was what she was looking for in a job, then she would just go and see an agency.

The waiter walked up to her table at this time. "Will there be anything else, miss?"

Skylar looked up and smiled at him. "No, there's nothing else. Tell the cook it was a lovely meal which I enjoyed very much today." After being handed her check, she laid down enough money for her meal and a good tip.

Stepping out into the bright sunlight caused a momentary blindness. So Skylar never saw what was coming at her and wasn't able to defend herself. After feeling something connect with her jaw, all she knew was that blackness was beginning to engulf her.

Nobody noticed what was taking place; it would have seemed as though the young lady had tripped. And the man was helping her so she didn't fall and get hurt.

Knowing he had accomplished the look he had wanted, Rhys caught her before she hit the pavement. He then proceeded to carry his burden to the car. Upon reaching the car, Craig jumped out to open the door.

Once settled inside, Rhys spoke, "Craig dial Alan's number for me."

Craig handed the phone into the backseat after dialing the number. "It's ringing."

"Hello. This is Dr. Alan Cantrell's residence, may I help you?" the housekeeper asked.

"Helen, this is Rhys. Could I speak with Alan?"

"One moment please, I'll get him."

Alan came to the phone a minute later. "Rhys! What do I owe for the privilege of a call in the middle of the afternoon? Surely you're not just calling to pass the time of day? That would be unheard of."

Rhys sighed very loudly, and took a deep breath that Alan recognized as anger.

"Sorry little brother, it sounds as though you could use a spot of humor today. Well, what can I do for you?" Alan asked.

"I found her."

Alan had no need to ask whom. "Where, and what are you going to do about it?"

"That's why I'm calling. I need to talk with you about a few things, but I don't want to get into it over the phone. Where we found her isn't important, she's in the car with us now. We're just pulling into your drive this moment, so I'll talk to you in the house."

When the car finally pulled up to the front door of Alan's house, Rhys spoke to the other two in the car. "Stay with her. I doubt that I'll be very long. Better check with the airport, and have them get the plane ready. And call the pilot and have him there on standby. Make sure she doesn't wake up and try to get out while you're waiting on me."

Walking up to the door, Rhys raised his hand to knock. But Alan had it open before he even had the chance. There was no need for greetings between the brothers. Alan led the way to his den, and Rhys followed. Once they had a bit of privacy, Alan proceeded to get them both a drink, knowing they would probably have need of it. It also gave him something to do while he was waiting for Rhys to begin.

"I'm taking her back out to the ranch. I want her to be sedated, just until we get there. Can you help me?"

Alan looked at his brother. "That isn't ethical, but I'm your brother, so yes I'll help you. Are you sure you don't want her sedated a little longer? Once you guys get out to the ranch, and sit down, everything is going to start to set in. Then you're going to need time to consider just what you want to do with her.

"Right now, you're operating on pure adrenalin. I think maybe there might even be a part of you that's in shock, while the other part of you is feeling numb. So I'm telling you, you are going to need time to think through your actions. Believe what I'm telling you."

Turning and glaring at his brother, Rhys said, "You want me to think some more? I've had five long years to think. Get real Alan!"

Knowing he had to make his brother see some sense, Alan tried again. "After you get out to the ranch, you'll sit down and try to unwind, but I know you too well. Everything is going to start to run through your mind. We all know what you're like when you lose that temper of yours. You need to have your head on straight, not up your ass, before there is any confrontation with Bree. You really need to be in control first, before you start anything.

"I realize you've been living in hell for the last five years. Longer if you consider the problems the two of you were having before her disappearance. Please, I'm asking you as your brother, as well as your friend, to think first. Consider everything very carefully, but for God's sake, and your mortal soul, think first before you act. I can't stress this enough.

Slumping down onto the couch, Rhys realized what his brother was getting at. Then he sighed. "I know you're right, Alan. But there is so much running through my head right now. I haven't even talked to Dad yet. Could you give him a call while I'm heading to the ranch?"

"Good, I'm glad what I've been saying is finally sinking in. I'll get you a couple sedatives; they are the same kind that Bree took before so I know it is okay for her. They last about six hours, just dissolve them in some water. It will be easier to get them into her, that way."

Alan walked Rhys out to the car and took a look into the back seat. "She still looks the same. Doesn't appear to be any change at all. She certainly held her age well? I wonder if her disposition is any different." He was also wondering to himself, as to what had really caused his sister-in-law to just take off all those years ago – then to just come back to the same town now. He didn't understand.

Rhys had been looking at his wife, and then, turning back to his brother, he said, "She does look the same, doesn't she? And I couldn't really say for sure what she's like anymore. But she'll find out soon enough that I've changed." Anger was entering his voice again. "I don't care about her any longer. I just want to know what she did with our child."

Alan placed his hand on Rhys's arm. "Remember what we just talked about. I want you to take care. If you think you need me for anything, call. I'll jump on the first flight out." Looking into the front seat he said, "You two try to keep him from doing something he will regret later. I'll call Dad when I go back in. Again, take care."

Rhys was embracing his brother. "I know," he murmured. Turning back to the car, Rhys crawled in and told himself to relax. "Let's go"

On the way to the airport, it remained quiet in the car. Rhys put a pill into Bree's mouth and let it melt. The taste would be awful when she woke, but that was just too bad.

Rhys wanted to remember and think on what had happened. He could remember it all this way now, because he knew what most of the facts really were. Having found *Bree's* diary, reading it from cover to cover over the last five years, he knew it like the back of his hand. He spent the car ride to the airport, and the flight to the ranch, thinking over the events of his life that included his long-lost wife.

★★★

Bree Anna Landon was thinking over everything her father had told her. He wanted – no needed – this merger with the Cantrells. Matt had told her they were almost broke; there could be no more traveling or huge parties. This way of life would be over unless she was willing to help with his plan. She was to get Rhys Cantrell to fall in love with her. That way, if or when anything happened, Rhys wouldn't press charges when he found out how worthless their company was.

After losing his wife, Matt's heart hadn't been in the business, and he let others control the company. They made bad choices, which had brought them to this desperate point.

So here she sat, with a photo of the man, and a brief report about him. If the picture did him any justice at all, Rhys Cantrell could only be described as drop-dead-gorgeous. His hair was dark and wavy and it looked so thick that it seemed to cry out to be touched. Then there was a slow smirk on his face – she imagined it could melt most hearts. And those eyes! What would it be like to drown in them? They would probably absorb your very soul. Their color had to be described as turquoise, and they seemed to sparkle with hidden and secret knowledge.

Laying the photo aside, Bree leaned back in her chair and began fantasizing about being with this man. Would reality be as good as the thoughts that were going through her head? It was going to be quite an adventure finding out. But the fantasies usually ended up disappointing her, didn't they? Why couldn't she feel anything in real life? It was like there was nothing on the inside since her mother died hating her father. Had the hatred her mother felt for Matt cause Bree Anna to feel disappointment in her own relationships?

She finally picked the report up to read. If the gossip was to be believed, then Rhys had left a string of broken hearts all over the place. And they said he started breaking those hearts when he was only sixteen.

Besides breaking hearts, he had started working in his father's business directly after college, and was going strong at it. He was doing things by leaps and bounds. And the women loved it, he just tired of them quickly.

He had lost his mother years ago; it seemed to have been hard on the whole family. A very close-knit family, seemingly sharing their thoughts and actions constantly and easily with one another. What would that be like?

There were two brothers, a cousin, and father ... could she fool them all?

The older brother, name of Alan, studied to be a doctor, set up a practice, married recently, and was expecting his first child. The younger was named Ethan. He was college bound, unsure of which direction to take in the future, but was probably going into the family business, with no impediments at present. The cousin's name was Craig Stien: same age as youngest brother, college bound, no serious relationship, orphaned at age four when his parents were killed in an accident. They had all grown up together, making them very close. They were always closing ranks when needed to help each other.

Turning to the next section of the report, she continued reading about Rhys. Maybe it was time to read a few of the newspaper and magazine excerpts, she thought with a laugh. The more she knew, the better for their plans. One part of an article caught her attention more than any of the others.

It stated that Rhys expected honesty and virtue in his prospective bride. When asked if he would give out her name, it was said all he did was throw back his head and roar with laughter. Then he turned to the reporter, and made the following remark:

"I haven't even met her yet. But I know she's out there, and when we meet, we'll be married so fast, there will be no question of her getting away from me."

Shaking her head, Bree put the article aside; it was time to think this through. Could she do what her father wanted? But really, how could she not? If she wanted to keep living the lifestyle she was used too, she had to help her father. What would it be like, to have a man such as Rhys Cantrell in love with her, and could she love him in return? She was sure she could make Rhys fall in love with her, but to reciprocate that love? Impossible.

Why couldn't she feel things like others? But, even without reciprocal love, the rewards would undoubtedly be ten-fold, if she could pull it off. In fact, her mother had done the same for years. Hadn't she?

★★★

The Cantrells all arrived about the same time. Brandon Cantrell had asked them all to attend this dinner party. He wanted to come tonight as a family united, not only in business, but also united in each other's best interests.

Once all were assembled, Brandon gave a short speech. "Thanks for coming boys, we don't get together near enough nowadays. That's one of the reasons I wanted you all with me, and I miss you guys. You each have a life of your own but we never forget family, even when we are all going in different directions."

Each of them nodded, they knew exactly what their father meant.

Brandon was looking his boys over – some of them were smartasses, (really men now), before going into the Landon's. He was wondering where all the years had gone.

Alan was the oldest, he had always wanted to be a doctor. He finally had his dream, and he was settling into his own practice quite nicely. He had a lovely wife, even if she was a bit head-strong at times, and wouldn't listen to his advice. And there was a child on the way. This being the first grandbaby, he had big plans for this child. He would spoil it to no end, as would be his right as the grandfather and all.

"How's that wife of yours, Alan? I hope she's feeling better? She has to take care of herself. I want my first grandbaby to born right."

Alan grinned at his father. "She's doing just fine, dad. After all, she is married to a doctor." His dad had seemed more worried than either him or his wife over this pregnancy. He was always fussing about what she might be "over-doing" as he would say.

Then came Rhys, he had just wanted to help out in the business from the time he was a young boy, but Brandon had made him get a degree first. Who knew he would actually have a real flare for business? One day soon, no doubt, he would be in the driver's seat of the company. He was a real go getter, that boy. No permanent lady in his life for now, but there was plenty of time for a lady-love.

Ethan was next in line, he was going to college for now, undecided. No definite plans for the future, as yet. If he didn't lean towards anything, Brandon knew he would come back to the family fold, per say. He needed to have some fun for now; responsibilities come soon enough, so there was no sense in rushing it.

His nephew, Craig, who was only a few months younger than Ethan, was next in line. Brandon had raised him with his own sons, so he was as much a son as the rest. When his sister and husband had been killed, it was all he had left of her. Craig was going to the same college as Ethan, no doubt with some of the same plans in mind. He was just having fun as well, but he knew, just like Ethan, when to get serious.

In a few years, Brandon figured that he would get them interested in joining the family business, if nothing else cropped up. He took one last look at the young men that were standing before him. He was so proud of his boys, and knew their mother would have been also. He loved them more than life itself.

So, nodding his head, he led the way up to their host's front door.

Inside, there was a lot of small talk going on, which made Rhys restless. He had told the brothers to keep their eyes and ears open, just in case.

There was something missing in Rhys's life: a partner to share things with, to go home to. Alan always looked happy now; having a wife seemed to give him everything he could have asked for. Rhys thought that it was time to think of finding himself a wife. But he didn't want to settle, she would need to be as nice as his mother had been, or a woman like Chelsea, Alan's wife. It was time to start thinking, and looking.

But where to find a good woman? *That* was the question of the hour. Seventy-five percent of the women Rhys knew wore different masks for all the different occasions. Could he find a genuinely warm, loving, and giving one? Were there any women like that left in their circle, or should he look elsewhere? He wanted someone to want *him*, not the money or family name.

He wanted this dinner over. He had things to do, like getting back to the office to finish up a few things so he could take off for the weekend.

He hadn't been crazy about this merger his father wanted. Something was off. It was all too compact. His instincts told him that they were missing a vital piece of information. Rhys had hopes that his father would see or hear something tonight to make him take a step back and reconsider things. If not, and his father was satisfied, the merger would, most likely, go ahead.

Impatiently, Rhys was wondering what the hold up with dinner was. They should have sat down thirty minutes ago. Just about to inquire as to why, there was a stir over by the doorway. Looking up with the others, he was positive that a goddess was entering the room. He was taking it all in: tall and slender, but not overly so. When the crowd parted for her, he saw long, long legs, and hair that was a lustrous blonde. No, he had to change his mind; words didn't come close. What did her hair remind him of?

Suddenly he knew, it was spun gold, with traces of…strawberries. That was as close as he could say, and that was it. Spun gold, mixed with ripe, luscious strawberries.

Trying to get a closer look at her face, to see if it matched the body, he wondered if she would be like the rest. Would her personality match up to her looks, or was it just surface beauty? He hoped not. But one thing was for sure, he was going to try and get to know her this evening Rhys was already thinking she was going to be his … where did that come from? Rhys wanted, no, needed, to get closer to her.

Alan looked at him, and then shook his head, beginning to laugh at his brother's expression. Rhys was a goner and just didn't know it yet. "It looks as though another of the musketeers is ready to fall," Alan murmured with a chuckle.

This brought Rhys' head back around to face his brothers. Looking them each in the eyes, he gave them all one of those shitty grins he was famous for. Then nodded because he knew what Alan meant.

"Remember, it's all for one, and one for all Rhys." Ethan reminded his brother, with a grin of his own, just to get a poke in.

"Not this time, little brother." Turning, Rhys walked over to where his father was standing. "Dad, the young woman who just arrived a few moments ago, who is she?"

Brandon knew that look all too well; he had it on his own face when he had first meet his wife, and so, with a chuckle, he told his son who it was. "That, my boy, is Bree Anna Landon, our host's only daughter. So you be nice, just not too nice. You hear me? I don't want you getting any ideas. I've heard she's pretty innocent, been away at school these last years. She's not used to all this attention, so you go easy."

Brandon hoped Rhys had heard what he said. He didn't want things to mess up this merger; this company had great potential if the right people were running it, not the clowns who were doing it now. He wanted nothing to disrupt his plans with Matt at this point.

Rhys found himself sitting next to the lady in question during dinner. She didn't seem to really notice him, which surprised and angered him at the same time. What was wrong with her? Maybe he should take his father's advice, and go easy and get to know her. But how could he get to know her if he couldn't get her to talk to him?

There seemed to be something there, though. Damn! He couldn't even keep his mind on the food. Or for that matter, keep his eyes where they should be. Not to mention that his pants where getting uncomfortable by just sitting so close to her. His meal went almost untouched, which was saying something, because nothing had ever affected his eating habits before. If there was something Rhys liked as much as women, it was his meal. Food was a passion for his family, and especially for him. His mother had taught him well in that regard.

After everyone had finished their meal, it was decided they would linger over drinks and socialize for a time. Rhys started looking around the room for her. Where was she? He had never before searched a room for a certain woman; they always sought him out. It was a strange feeling, being the hunter, instead of the hunted.

He spotted her across the room, talking to another man. For some unknown reason, this angered him to no end. Could he be jealous? Surely not this soon? He didn't even know this woman yet, but here he was thinking of her as his very own.

Suddenly, Bree looked up, and her eyes seemed to lock with his. Neither could seem to look away, even if they had wanted to. Rhys and Bree were connecting, and it was like an electrical bond forming. Was this just chemistry, or something much bigger? Then, someone stepped between them, breaking that connection. Rhys began walking across the room directly toward her. Bree turned away as she was asked a question, but she seemed hesitant to turn away from him.

Being behind Bree was even better. Rhys decided to lean over and whisper his idea for them into her ear. "How would you like to get out of here? We could go for a drive out towards the beach."

Bree shivered with reaction to Rhys's voice. She couldn't believe it. Could it be possible that this wasn't going to be as hard as she first thought? However, she hadn't been prepared for her own reaction to this man. This was going to be a very pleasant interlude after all. She turned to him and looked into his eyes. She sighed softly, "Yes, I'd like to very much. Let me just go and speak to my father."

For the first time tonight, Rhys was able to see the color of Bree's eyes. They had to be the most beautiful green he had ever seen. They took his breath away – the color reminded him of the purest jade.

Taking ahold of her hand, they walked together toward Matt, but Matt just nodded his head. It was okay for them to leave. Rhys led the way into the night, and reaching the car, he opened the door. He decided that they would drive along the coast and then end up at the Cantrell beach house.

There was companionable silence during their drive as neither seemed to want to talk. Both were thinking about how they wanted to proceed with this situation. Bree was thinking about how she actually wanted this man, her need for him having a mind of its own. How had this happened? She didn't normally fall under men's spells like this, or so fast. Bree was sure she couldn't be falling for Rhys, but she couldn't help thinking that maybe, just maybe, a happily ever after was possible for her after all…but they hadn't even shared a kiss as yet.

She was going to have to watch her step here, which was going to be the hardest thing that she had tried lately. She wasn't going to be able to fool this man very easily. After all, he wasn't like any man she had ever met before. Could she get him to fall for her, without losing herself? Being unsure of a man was something new to her. Before she had always been able to get any man she wanted, or get them to do what she wanted.

If he did fall for her, would the past matter so much? Bree guessed maybe she should keep that part of her life hidden for the time being. What was it the reporters had said? A virtuous woman – yes that was what he wanted, so that's what he would get from her.

Bree wondered how much longer it would be until they got to where they were going. What would happen after they got there? Bree was hoping things would progress with a rapid pace, but knew she couldn't allow it to.

Beside her and behind the wheel, Rhys still couldn't believe his luck. He hadn't had to coax her or even use his unfailing charm on her. He had just asked her, and here they were leaving her father's dinner party behind them. Maybe he should pinch himself, just to see if he was day-dreaming.

She had to have felt the attraction as much as he had. She had been bold there in a room full of people, but now, she seemed shy and innocent. Should he do the right thing, talk to her, get to know her before trying to proceed any further? It was the right thing, after all – what his father had asked him to do – but he wasn't sure he could proceed with caution. Was she like all the rest, just playing along for all it was worth, hoping to get his money rather than his love, or was she for real? Could he chance this? A relationship with her could be a dangerous undertaking. He could lose himself completely to her, and then his heart would more than likely be lost forever, not to mention the implications for the family business.

Finally, the beach house drive was coming into sight. Rhys turned to look at his passenger. The two hour drive had given him time to think. It was too dark in the car, so he couldn't read her face, but with so much electricity floating through the car, Rhys felt like a school kid again and hoped she felt the same way. If they didn't get out of the car soon, he would probably try to get her to make out like a teenager.

Needing to slow things down a bit, Rhys threw his door open. He got out and took a few deep breaths. Deciding a walk on the beach would help cool him off, so he looked across the car roof and said, "Come on, I think a walk is just what we both need."

Going around the car, Bree had another idea. She walked right into his arms and reached up to touch his face. "Kiss me first. I want to see if this is only my imagination. I have to know if this feeling is going to go away, or be there for both of us. Do you understand what I'm trying to say?"

Lowering his head, Rhys let his lips touch hers. The kiss started out as a test. It was like no first kiss either of them had ever experienced before. They both felt their hearts take flight. Finally, Rhys pulled himself away. Damn, he had almost forgotten why he wanted to go for a walk in the first place. He had wanted to slow things down, but after just one kiss, he was lost.

With a passionate, heavy voice, Bree tried to speak. "I – I think maybe a walk after all. I got the answer to my question, plus a whole lot more."

CHAPTER 5

THINKING THE SUBJECT SHOULD BE changed, she went on talking. "The beach is beautiful washed in moonlight tonight. Don't you think?"

Knowing exactly what she was trying to do, all Rhys could do was go along with her. "Yes, it is. But do you really want to talk about trivial things, when we know nothing about each other? I want to know everything about you before this night is through."

They began walking down the beach, talking about anything that popped into their heads. It was getting harder and harder to keep out of each other's arms. They were desperately trying to hold their passion at bay, but it was becoming a losing battle. They were stopping more frequently to share kisses, which were fast rising to an intense level.

Rhys felt that he would die if they didn't make love soon. He didn't want this first time to be on a sandy beach; he thought this woman deserved so much more. Taking her hand, he led her back the way they had come. With the house in view, Rhys knew no one would bother them while they were there, and so he couldn't help grinning at what he knew would soon happen between them.

Upon entering the house, Rhys found Bree moving into his arms once more. It seemed neither could get enough of the other, both aroused to the point of wanting to rip each other's clothes off. Bree pulled back slightly, looking up into Rhys's eyes. "Oh Rhys, what has happened to me? We only met hours ago, but it feels like I've known you always. All I can think of is being with you till the end of time. Tell me you feel the same way, too."

Looking into those passion-filled eyes, Rhys would have told her just about anything. But all he could think of at this point was shutting her up. "You talk too much woman, come here." He started to kiss her senseless. Breathlessly he pulled away. Then, sweeping Bree up into his arms, Rhys went up the stairs. Going in the room, he kicked the door shut with the back of his foot.

Ever so slowly, he let her slide down the entire length of his body. He wanted to feel each and every part of that luscious body against his. It was heaven, and hell combined. Not able to stand the wait any more, he started removing her clothes, piece by piece. Rhys had intentions to enjoy this more than he had ever enjoyed it before. Gently, he guided her back towards the bed. Laying her down, he paused to look upon her while removing his own clothing.

When he laid down beside her, they began kissing anew. Running their hands over each other's bodies, trying to discover the secret places that before had been hidden by clothes. Suddenly, Bree was whimpering to him. "Rhys … Rhys, please help me."

Rhys had been almost beyond having any control left. He barely heard her. Was she saying what he thought she was implying? Taken aback, he couldn't believe what was registering in his mind. Had he heard right or not? He was totally unsure. Pulling away slightly, he looked down into her face, to see what was there. "Are you saying, that you've never been with a man before?"

Bree just stared at him, not saying anything.

"Answer me Bree. Dammit, answer me." Rhys growled. He shook her, displeased to be waiting for an answer at a time like this.

Pulling away, Bree grabbed a robe that had been lying at the foot of the bed. Getting up, she needed to put the room between them. Space was what she needed. She had better think up something fast to try and explain. "Rhys, I don't understand what's wrong with you. You are scaring me by acting this way! Of course I haven't been with anyone before this. I was waiting for the right man to come into my life. After all we talked about and shared this night, then coming back here, I can't believe you could even ask me this. What kind of person do you think I am?"

With tears running down her face, she went on. "Was I totally wrong, or did I imagine you felt the same. When I said I wanted to be with you till the end of time, what did you think I was talking about? I was very serious about it, I thought you felt the same."

Rhys felt stunned by all of what he was hearing, what could he say, how to put his thoughts into words.

Bree's face became red with her anger. "Oh, that's right, you didn't answer me, did you? You just kissed me to shut me up, was that it? I must have been crazy to think you were someone special. And where do you get your nerve, getting angry with me? I willingly was giving you everything tonight."

Bree walked over to stare out the window, trying not to sob out loud. Why didn't he say something, anything? It would be better than this silence. Had she ruined her chances with him – was everything lost now? What would she tell her father? He wouldn't accept failure from his daughter! Combining all the sorrow and anger she was feeling, her voice quivered. "When I first saw you, it was like I was free-falling off the side of a mountain. I was having fantasies, even before we met, just from having seen you across the room.

"Then when you finally kissed me for the first time, I thought *this is it*. I had died and gone to heaven. But then, maybe I'm a fool. Thoughts like this probably never entered into your mind. I wonder, did they?" Giving a loud sob, Bree wrapped her arms around herself, and put all the bitterness of anger into her words. "This was all a game to you, wasn't it? You just had to see if the great Rhys Cantrell could get yet another woman into your bed! You're like every other man around aren't you?"

With that, she started crying harder while gathering up her clothes to get dressed.

Rhys couldn't stand it anymore. She was so wrong! He had sounded angry due to being surprised that she was untouched and afraid that he could have hurt her. He had stayed silent because he couldn't believe that God had entrusted this woman to him. That she had saved herself and thought enough of him that she was willing to gift him with her virginity was almost too much for him to bear. There could be no greater gift to a man than this. Not caring about his nudity, Rhys got off the bed and went over to her. Bree continued to keep her back to him, while trying to dress. Standing right behind her, he paused to get his thoughts straight. He had to make her understand why he had acted the way he had, why he had seemed so angry. "Bree, stop, please. Look at me."

She did stop then, but didn't turn toward Rhys yet. If she gave in too soon, the game might be lost. Rhys tried again. "Bree, sweetheart, you don't realize this, but I could have hurt you. I was so far gone, I wasn't thinking of being gentle."

When he went to take her arm to turn her, he saw that she stiffened. This caused him to drop his hands back down to his sides. But he knew he had to go on. "I almost had no control left – the passion you had aroused in me was so great. Dammit, I wanted to take you so fast and hard, it would have made your head spin.

"I know you probably don't want to believe this, but I do still want you. But you deserve to have gentleness your first time, and I was feeling anything but gentle, I assure you. Can you understand now? I was angrier with myself than with you. I felt a great loathing for the way in which I had planned on taking you. I'm sorry I took it out on you. Can you find it in your heart to forgive me … do you think?"

Reaching out once more, he turned Bree around this time. Lifting her face, he saw the tears that were running down. Knowing he had put them there was like a kick to the stomach. Maybe this woman would be the real thing. To find such a gift just when he was thinking of finding someone, it had to be destiny, didn't it?

Sighing, Rhys pulled her against his chest, needing to hug her close. "Oh Bree! I think I may have just fallen in love with you." Did he say that out loud? Did he care? Leaning down, he kissed her gently, feeling he had to show her that he could cherish her. There wasn't passion in this kiss, it was to ask for forgiveness, to try and fix her tears.

It hit Rhys, then and there, that he had found someone that he could picture as his wife – and to think that they had only met hours before! The fact she was Matt Landon's daughter would make his own father happy. With this merger pending, it could tip the scales and finalize the decision.

Lifting her chin once again and looking into her eyes, Rhys asked hesitantly, "Will you marry me, my dear Bree? Now. Tonight. We'll fly to Vegas, if your answer is yes."

"Oh Rhys." Bree leaned up on her tip-toes, and kissed him full on the lips. Then, she sighed and threw her head back and happily shouted her answer. "YES!"

Gathering his woman into his arms, Rhys began spinning her around. This woman was soon to be his wife, but not soon enough for him. They shared a kiss filled with all the promised passion to come.

Dressing quickly, they raced for the airport. While on the plane, Rhys made all the arrangements for their wedding. He called a small private chapel, not wanting to wait in line behind others. Then the fun could start after they got to the bridal suite in the hotel. He held Bree in his arms the whole trip, afraid she might disappear before his eyes. All he could do was hope this night wasn't just a dream.

Arriving in Vegas, there was a car waiting at the airport to take them on their adventure. They found themselves married within fifteen minutes after arriving. Neither could wait to get to the hotel. On the drive back across town, it was hard for Rhys to remember he had to go slow with her. If it wasn't for the fact that she was a virgin, he would have wanted to pull off and start right now. This woman was going to be his at last.

He needed to calm down. Taking a few deep breaths and thinking about how they had forever helped him. Bree wasn't going anywhere.

Meanwhile, Bree's thoughts were going a mile a minute. What was she going to do? He would know soon enough that she had lied to him, because she wasn't a so-called virgin. Damn, why had she agreed to marry him so fast? The simple reason was due to the fact she couldn't help herself. She really wanted him for her own, and this was how she wanted it to end. They were almost to the hotel, and she couldn't let Rhys guess before the marriage was consummated. Something would come to her, wouldn't it?

While riding the elevator to the top floor, it came to her. She would think like a virgin. She had seen enough movies, even if she couldn't remember what it had been like her first time. It had been many years and men ago, so let's hope she would get it right. The key was showing reluctance at the beginning now. Maybe feign surprise, but no, that wouldn't work after what had happened just hours earlier in the evening.

Well, why not just show her eagerness to finally be together? Yes, that's what she would do. Act shy upon entering the room, and show just the right amount of nervousness.

After tipping the bellboy, Rhys turned and saw how nervous Bree was. Did she think he was going to just jump her? No wonder, after the way he had acted earlier. Well, it was time to be the man his father raised – he knew how to be patient, and earn her trust again.

Rhys went across the room to Bree. "Do you need to relax a bit? We could have a glass of champagne or a bite to eat? Your call. I want you to get your nerves settled so you can be at ease."

"No, I mean…I'm alright. I'm just a little unsure of myself. Maybe a glass of champagne is what I need."

Rhys poured them both a drink and they sat on the sofa. After a couple of minutes, Rhys took their glasses and placed them on the coffee table. Gently, he took her into his arms and began kissing her fears away. It was becoming increasingly difficult to hold back, as Bree was getting just as eager as Rhys himself was.

The passion was released from their bonds of restraint, and reaching the bed seemed like an impossibility. Their first love making was going to end up on the floor in front of the fire-place. Clothes were removed quickly, and both were naked before either realized it. Sinking to the floor, hands seemed to roam at will, inflaming them beyond limits.

Ever so slowly, Rhys was spreading her thighs; he wanted her ready for his entry. Running his hands up and down the inside of her legs, he was teasing, letting his fingers brush over her lightly. Finally he began lowering himself onto her, letting her accept his weight. He was close, so close to entering her. Should it be in one thrust, getting the pain over, and how much pain would there be? Maybe slowly, letting her stretch little by little, he couldn't wait any longer. Damn, with a swift thrust he entered her sheath. But wait, where was the barrier he had heard that you felt when entering a virgin? She didn't act like there was any pain.

Damn! Did she lie after all?

Before he could think on this further, his passion took over. They both were going over the edge, like falling into a field of fireworks.

Rhys laid there holding Bree; afterward was just as important as the actual love making to him. Wrapped in each other's arms, Rhys was feeling satiated. Snuggling and kissing, then just holding each other, Rhys thought back to his entry. A few doubts were creeping back into his mind. "Did I hurt you, sweetheart?" Rhys asked.

Feeling very content, Bree answered honestly. "No. But never in my wildest dreams did I think that it would, or could, be like this." And then it was like someone threw a glass of ice water on her as it dawned on her as to why he had asked about hurting her. She had to think fast – needed an explanation to his inquiry.

"Rhys, can I ask you something important?"

Rhys figured he already knew what she was about to come out with, so he nodded yes, so they could get it over with.

"Will you be wanting children?" With a quiver in her voice she continued. "I mean do you think, you might in the future?" When Rhys went to talk, Bree placed her fingers over his lips to quiet him. "Please, let me finish first. We should have talked about this before we got married, but it was all happening so fast. I didn't even think about it."

Choking herself up, she went on. "I … I had an accident when I was young, I was only twelve at the time it happened. I really don't want to talk about the actual accident, because it brings back a lot of bad memories for me. But, the doctors ended up having to give me an internal examination at that time. They told me I would probably be all right, but there was no guarantees of the fact." Bree began to sob, unable to finish her thoughts, and then made as though she was going to get up from Rhys's arms.

Rhys pulled Bree back, and then he started to rock her as he would a small child. Holding her there, he was plagued by his conscience. There he had been thinking she was about to tell him some sordid past. He began to wonder what kind of accident she had had, and whether or not she should see a doctor in the near future to see if there were any lingering problems.

"Bree, as long as there no problems with us, don't worry. Your health is important to me, now you're my wife, and I would never endanger you with a pregnancy if it would cause you any harm. Don't hide things, just talk to me and we will work out whatever it is in the future.

"If it's alright, if we want children in the future, we will talk to a doctor before we try. If you can't have a child, we can adopt or use a surrogate if it comes to that." He held her closer and she breathed a sigh of relief and hid her face in the crook of his neck and shoulder.

"Everything will work out in time, you'll see. Now enough of these tears – this is our honeymoon, isn't it?" Rhys hoped that he had reassured Bree as to how he felt, and put her mind at ease.

CHAPTER 6

A FEW DAYS LATER, THEY decided it was time to go home. The merger had probably gone through while they were away, so their families would be even happier about their circumstances. Even though they hadn't shared the actual ceremony with them, Rhys knew they would be throwing a big party in their honor. Rhys sent text messages to all his family telling them what had occurred. Then shut off his phone so they could be alone for a bit longer before the real world intruded.

Little did Rhys know, there was to be no party to celebrate their marriage. His family was not overjoyed to have the Landons as part of the family at this time − a discovery Rhys was soon to learn of.

There was trouble almost from the beginning of the merger; they found things had been ingeniously arranged so as to hide many facts. Records were being unearthed, which showed all had not been disclosed. The records were headed to the shredder, but one of the former employees had a grudge against Matt, so he lifted them. He gave them to the new owners, hoping they would back out of the deal or press charges.

There was a great, unknown debt that the Cantrell business would have to absorb. Matt's business had only been hanging on by a thread. A great number of the company assets had been mortgaged to the hilt. Matt should have tried to gain control of his company again after his wife's death, and maybe see if someone could help. Instead, to hide so much, he had spent countless hours in negotiations to keep his employees quiet. What else would the Cantrell solicitors find in the weeks to come? If anything, they knew trouble was ahead for them all.

It was decided that a small dinner party would still have to be held for the newlyweds, whether anyone liked it or not. Rhys had stressed it wasn't Bree's fault as it didn't appear she had ever had anything to do with her father's business, and he needed to honor his wife as a new member of their family. Oh, how little he knew about the Landon's scheme.

Rhys hadn't been back in the office for more than a week when things went from bad to worse. The creditors were clamoring for their money now that the Cantrells had taken possession of the business. Everyone had heard the news and wanted their share now. No one wanted to wait and see if the Cantrells could pull this business out of the red.

They all knew what was going through each other's head, but no one was willing to voice the thoughts out loud. This merger was going to cost them; they had spent years building their business and reputation. How long would it take them to pull the fat from the fire on this one?

Rhys was working harder than ever – he needed to pull things together and make this merger viable. He had to travel, and bring new accounts in to build up one side of the business to help out the other side. Little by little, progress began to be seen by the family.

But due to all the extra work required, Rhys wasn't able to spend as much time with his new wife as he wanted to. They had been married three months when Bree began to complain that she was always alone. Why couldn't one of his brothers do some of the things he was doing? She wanted to enjoy some time with him and not just sit at home. Bree began going to parties without her husband, and she felt justified in doing so due to being ignored by him so often.

How could she have thought her life was going to be made? Why had her father not told her how bad things were? Why did he wimp out of the business when her mother died? He should have been able to make things even better without having to worry about a wife! Did that make her sound hateful? Well, she didn't care! Her life should be easy now, but she never got to see her husband. Even the money was tight because of the merger. She felt depressed, which wasn't how things should be.

It was her own fault for going along with her father's plan. How would she make this right with her husband? Had she really fallen in love with him? He probably hated her more than anyone in this world because of her family's lies, which had to be the reason why he was trying so hard to bring this part of the business back to where it should be.

Rhys found that Bree was hardly ever at home when he did manage to be there. Why couldn't she understand that he felt somewhat responsible for this situation? If he had been more vocal about his concern to his father, insisted on more time to look into things, maybe things would be different right now.

Something had to be done. Their marriage wasn't going to last how things stood now. Their relationship had to change. It wasn't just going to be the two of them struggling for footing anymore. He had found a home pregnancy stick that showed Bree was pregnant. Having thought they would probably never have a child, this discovery changed things. With a baby coming, this should bring them closer, but Bree seemed angry about it. Rhys knew she had been drinking heavily and often; he found her passed out on more than one occasion. Rhys didn't want to admit that he suspected that Bree didn't always come home at night when he was away on business. It had only been nine months and things were falling apart at the seams.

Finally, one day, his father called him into the office. Things had gotten beyond the point of turning a blind eye to her stunts, for attention. "Sit down son, I want you to listen to some advice. Say nothing until I'm finished, Okay?" Brandon gave a serious look, and seeing Rhys would comply, continued reluctantly. He didn't want to hurt his son.

"We all realize, because of your marriage, you feel this overwhelming responsibility about what Matt pulled on us. But if you would stop and remember, it was my decision to go ahead with the deal. I wanted this company to be part of ours. Maybe that will show you we all make mistakes, but it was a good company at one time, and can be again. So, quit with the guilt trip. It is taking over your life. I do appreciate the extra work you've put in, but it has to stop.

"We will get there, and it doesn't have to be this year. When this is affecting your marriage, it's time to step back. You're on the point of losing your wife, to a great many different things. Bree is almost beyond control. You need to take her in hand before she does something irreparable to herself, or possibly your child. Finish up this present deal you're working on, but finish A.S.A.P. Do you understand? We are all concerned about this, so we'll try to keep an eye on her. Hand off what you can to others in your department, and get your head screwed back on. Take a leave of absence. I don't care how long. We will get through this as a family, but you have to take care of Bree and your child, first."

Brandon had just voiced out loud what Rhys himself had felt. Rhys sat and listened to all his father had to say, without uttering a sound. Things were pointed out which had hurt, but he knew they were true. It was time to get home and find out a few things and then make some plans. He had been thinking their life was over, but if there was a chance that they could start over, begin again...

Brandon recognized Rhys's hopes and fears, and looked to his son as he stood to leave. "I love you son."

Standing, he embraced his dad, and sighed. "Thank you. When I get everything arranged here today, I'm going home to talk with Bree. I think we should go out to the ranch and stay. Grandfather is always yelling that none of us come home enough. I hope we can straighten out some of our problems there. With no distraction, what else will there be for us to do?"

Rhys headed to his office to arrange all the things to be taken care of and hand off what he could. Rhys called home to tell Bree he was on his way, but there was no answer. Rushing home, Rhys threw open the door and called out, "Bree, I'm home." There was still no answer. Maybe she was lying down and had fallen into a deep sleep. Heading to the bedroom, expecting to find his wife, he was in for a surprise. The bed was empty.

Did she have a doctor's appointment today, then had decided to eat out or shop for the baby? After another hour, Rhys was calling around to find where Bree was. He found she had gone out to a party with friends. Should he go and get her, drag her home? No, as angry as he felt at this moment, that would be a mistake. "Damn!" Rhys knew nothing would change until they could get away from this crowd she hung out with. While Rhys waited for Bree to come home, he was thinking on things he overheard from friends about his wife's life before they got together.

He hadn't wanted to believe the rumors, so he had ignored them. But the story she told him…was it all lies? Yes. He should have listened to the rumors and sought council from his family and friends. He should have remembered that some of the women of their circle lied to get what they wanted, but he thought she was truly different. Grabbing the picture of his wife, he hurled it against the wall. "Where the hell are you, Bree?"

Pacing around, he shouted some more. "And who the hell are you with, or should I wonder how many?" Rhys dropped down on the sofa, putting his head down. He wondered if the child was even his. But this would get him nowhere. This baby was his, no doubt. He had one of those undeniable feelings of certainty.

He would sit here and wait for Bree to return home, then find out some truths. Finally, he heard the key in the lock. He looked at his watch only to discover it was well into morning. Past two o'clock.

Bree was trying to shush whoever had brought her home. Would she never learn? She must have noticed the lamp burning, and assumed the housekeeper left it on for her. Why was she trying to sneak into her own home?

Rhys spoke with barely controlled anger. "Bree Cantrell, just where in hell have you been all night?"

Clearly startled at hearing her husband's voice, she turned and stared at him. Bree seemed to have lost the knowledge of speech. After a moment, she gathered herself together. "Oh Rhys. Your … home, when … did … you … get … here?" Bree slurred.

Rhys looked through her. "I told you this had to stop, and you promised it would. Well, clearly, I can't believe anything you say. Can I? You refuse to heed what I've said in the past, so we'll see if actions speak louder than words to you. We had a lot of plans for us, once I got things back in line at the office. But you don't give a damn about anyone but yourself, do you? Do you even care about our child? We'll be flying out to Grandfather's ranch in Virginia tonight. And by the way, we'll be there until further notice. Do you understand?" Rhys ended his command in a raised voice.

Bree tried to speak, but her words seemed stunted. "But … Rhys … I can't … go out there … right … now … while I'm carrying … this …

child. I need ... to be close ... to my ... doctor. Just ... in case ... something ... should happen."

Rhys heard enough to understand the message. Rounding on her, Rhys tried to suppress the fury in his voice. "Damn you to hell, Bree!!! You are only worried you will be away from your friends and parties. If you had one thought for our child, then you wouldn't be acting the way you have, partying and getting drunk every chance you have."

Bree thought to speak again, but seeing this, Rhys turned away from her. Neither thought about talking any longer. Reaching over, he took Bree's arm and led her out the door to the car. He phoned Alan, to see if they could stop off to have him look over Bree before their trip.

Chapter 7

Alan checked Bree over, and said to Rhys. "She should be alright, that is if you can get her to take care of herself at least until the baby arrives. Rhys, I don't like to say this, but it's like she is trying to destroy herself for some reason. I doubt she is thinking straight, so, I'm going to give you a prescription for a mild sedative that can be filled on the way to the airport. But for God's sake, don't trust her with it. I would advise you to keep it on hand, you'll be needing it in the days to come."

Rhys's voice was choked when he tried to speak. "That's the reason we're going out to the ranch. You of all people know what's been going on, right from the start. I want this baby to have a chance at life. If we don't leave the city now, who knows? But I know there is no way in hell my child will make it if we don't."

They arrived at the ranch and Bree was shown immediately to their room. She decided she would lay down to rest, maybe she would be able to take Rhys on if she had time to pull herself together.

Neither wanted to be in the same room as each had to get their minds straightened out before they tried to work on the problems at hand. So, Rhys left the house. He needed to walk out the frustrations that were going around his head while Bree napped in one of the bedrooms.

The first week was a very strained affair for everyone. At five months pregnant, she was putting weight on and hated it, absolutely hated it. Her clothes didn't fit right anymore, she was showing, and thought everyone would be laughing. She told Rhys that she felt like one of those dumb cows in the pasture. Which caused him to burst into laughter. This didn't please Bree one bit; she became moodier by the day.

Bree was starting to feel trapped. Why couldn't they all leave her alone? She was feeling guilt over so many things, mostly from before their marriage. She was going to find Rhys right now and make him talk to her. She wanted things over. Why drag it out? Bree needed to get out of here. Feelings of suffocation were starting to overwhelm her. If only Rhys could love the real her, just a little, maybe it would be worth all the trouble. Entering the library, Bree stomped across the room.

Rhys was sitting at the desk doing the ranch books. His thoughts were in a jumble, things weren't going how he thought they would. Why couldn't they make things work? What would it take? Just thinking of getting back to the job on hand, he heard the door open. Rhys knew agitation when he saw it, once again. What the hell was wrong now?

"Rhys I want to talk to you right now." As he remained silent, Bree grew all the angrier. Stomping her feet and screaming at him, she went on, "I hate it here, do you hear me?"

Rhys thought he would let her temper play itself out. He was getting used to all the temper tantrums at this point.

"Damn you! Listen to me. Quit ignoring me, you bastard!" Bree was screaming.

A hysterical Bree was not a pretty picture to say the least. But without realizing it, she started spouting out the very secrets that she had been keeping from Rhys all this time. "You and your family are so stupid. My father laid the plans out for everything! All the groundwork was done long before I ever met you. I had a photo of you and your family, a file of all your lives. I knew your likes, and dislikes. Even down to what type of woman you were looking to marry. Daddy told me everything he thought I would need to know.

"I married you to keep my lifestyle, and to keep your family from bringing charges against my father if the truth came out. I know how much your family hates scandals. When you asked me to marry you, and the merger was sure to go through while we were away, I knew you wouldn't press charges against your new father-in-law. That whole must-save-the-family-name-at-all-costs bit.

"In reality it was for all your money, and prestige. You're nothing but a stupid dumb jerk, even though you're good looking, and a dream in bed."

Rhys was around the desk in seconds; it was too fast for Bree to step back. He had ahold of her and gave her a gentle shake. "I already knew all that garbage. You're not telling me anything I didn't already know. I'm not as stupid as you or your wonderful father would like to believe.

"I had you both investigated shortly after coming home from Vegas. I knew for a fact you were no virgin when we got married. And by the way, I knew there was no accident, causing the damage you said. But at that point I didn't care because you were my wife."

Seeing the look on Bree's face, Rhys continued. "I see you think I'm bluffing. Should we call up a few of your former lovers to prove my point?"

Bree was shaking her head.

"I didn't think it would be necessary."

Further disbelief entered her eyes, when it all finally registered. She tried to speak, but no words would come out at first. Trying again, she said. "Rhys, no."

"Yes, Bree."

"Rhys please, you couldn't even begin to understand. I can't deal with all the lies anymore. I have been carrying around so much guilt, and still am. I just wanted to try and forget everything, so I turned to drinking and partying."

Bree was crying as she slumped down on the couch. "It wasn't all lies. Rhys, I do really love you. It was only because of all the lies, that I said all those things to you." Leaving out another sob, she tried to go on. "It's that I hate myself. Trying to forget the way I trapped you into marriage. I didn't realize that we would end up falling in love."

Bree was crying uncontrollably now.

"Dammit Bree, I've been trying for so long to put the past where it belongs for our child's sake. But if you continue to lie, and act the shrew, what am I to do?"

Bree gasped. "I'm not lying this time, please believe me."

"I need to think, I'll be back." Not being able to handle anymore, Rhys turned and walked out. It was time to think on how to turn their lives around. The hell of it was, he still wanted to try and make things work for them so they could be a real family. It wasn't just for the sake of their child alone; there were genuine feelings for Bree herself. Even after all the lies and the partying and the backstabbing.

The following weeks had them tip toeing around each other. Neither wanted another confrontation like the last one. A few smiles passed between them, so a start had definitely begun.

Cousin Jordan showed up at the ranch. The family had only met him three years previously, due to the rift between Paul Sr. and Paul Jr that occurred with Jordan being born to a woman not Jr.'s wife. Once the two had made up, Jr. brought Jordan to the ranch when he was twenty-four. This was Paul Jr.'s only living child, and he wanted him to be part of the family before it was too late, so the meeting with the older Paul came about.

Sr. was a formidable man at most times, but he bent the harshness to accept this illegitimate grandchild. He couldn't hold anything against the son for what the father had done.

Jr. was dying, that was his one and only true reason for bringing his son out here. He wanted Jordan to have his rightful place in the family before he was gone. Jordan learned soon enough about Rhys's problems with his wife. One day he sought Rhys out to talk. "Rhys, I know we don't know each other well, but I would like to help if I can."

"Help? Just how the hell are you going to help? You're no doctor, are you?" Rhys found himself asking sarcastically.

Jordan sighed. "Rhys, listen. I've been working with troubled people for a while now. I'm studying to be a counselor, so in essence I might be able to help. You don't know about my life, or what I've been doing, so I can understand the mistrust. I know how to reach out to others, get them to open up. I can't promise anything, but Bree needs help dealing with her insecurities."

At Rhys's look, Jordan continued. "Yes she has insecurities whether you think so or not. She isn't as strong as you think. She needs to bring her whole self in alignment. I just finished helping a close friend come to terms with himself."

Rhys gave Jordan and skeptical look and turned to go. He didn't want to waste his time with some fool who thought he could help.

"You don't know what to think about us just popping back into the family. I understand, really I do. I only agreed to come out here to the ranch from time to time because of my father. It seems to mean a great deal to him. I'm more than ready to help if I can. You both could use help. Now, I can't promise anything or even fast results. But I am willing to try," Jordan finished.

Rhys didn't like to admit he needed help with Bree. If they were ever to be close again and be a family like he wanted, maybe this would be the answer. "Fine, I need help. Let's see what you can do. I do know it might not work, but heaven knows, we're getting nowhere this way. But if it does, I'll be eternally grateful."

Rhys continued to ponder his decision long after Jordan left to seek out Bree. At this point in time, things couldn't get any worse for them, or so he thought.

In the weeks to follow, Jordan and Bree spent lots of time talking. It seemed that he was drawing her back to her old self.

There just might be a ray of sunshine for them after all.

Even Rhys and Bree started to talk again. Jordan had told them they had to open up to work on a few problems at a time. They went on shopping trips, thoughtfully going over all the baby items in the different stores, wanting to buy just the right things. The talks and trips took on new meaning for them both. Things looked like they were going to be alright. They had to keep in mind that they had to keep things on an open scale.

Rhys and Bree talked a few weeks later, and they felt it was time for them to return to their own home. They wanted the baby to be born at the hospital close to their families, not hundreds of miles away. So the plans were made for the following week.

Being eight months pregnant, they decided to drive home instead of fly. It would give them more time to plan how things would be, and think about a family celebration. It would also be a deal safer for Bree. It had been a long time in coming, but everyone was glad that things had finally turned around. Rhys was on a high for two days, but reality set in too fast.

Just two days after making plans to travel home, on April 20, 2006, Bree was gone. She just was gone. No trace. It was as though she had disappeared entirely. She took absolutely nothing with her, not even any of the baby things. This made no sense at all – wouldn't she have taken at least something for the baby with her?

Rhys ripped their room apart trying to find a note – something, anything, to explain. How could she just be gone from his life, as if she had never been? It made no sense. None at all. The police investigated, checking into what they could, but with no clues as to which direction this case should go, it was as if their hands were tied. They were scrutinizing the history of the marriage. Could she have taken off on her own, fooling Rhys once again, or did the husband do away with her?

Paul Sr. watched his grandson sink deeper and deeper into despair. Why had the girl left so suddenly? They had begun rebuilding their life. Had she been afraid that something else might crop up to destroy it all? Nothing made sense at this point. Paul often found Rhys sitting in the nursery, going through all the baby items. This had to stop, but how could he wake the boy back up to life? He couldn't and wouldn't let it end like this.

Paul found himself wondering what to do, what kind of action to take with Rhys. He felt powerless, but also felt that he should be able to help stop the hurting. Paul called a friend, former FBI, and told him the story, asking if he could help in any way. The man said he would do all he could, but with nothing to go on, just looking over everything was the best he could offer.

Paul Sr. finally had a plan and it was time to get Rhys off his backside. Rhys needed to get mad, fight back, feel again, and take some action himself. With those thoughts in mind, Paul went in search of Rhys. He knew where he would be, sitting in that damn rocking chair in the nursery. Walking into the room, Paul said, "Rhys, its time you quit this damn sissified moping around."

Rhys started to speak. "Min –"

Paul quickly cut him off and continued. "Before you start yelling at me to mind my own business, you will sit there and let me have my say. You are someone who normally takes action, but what have you been doing? Just sitting around here going through this stuff, day after day. The police can't help. There isn't anything to go on.

"Where is the guy who digs until he can't dig anymore? It's time to hire a private detective to help and do work on the side the cops can't.

You need to get your mad on, use those Cantrell emotions, live your life and fight for this. Go and find her, boy. I don't think she fooled you. I saw her these last weeks, and it was real. So don't sit there and waste away in that there chair. A Cantrell never gives up a fight, now does he?

"I expected better out of you, you who fought like hell to save the company and get it back on track. You did, and a truer Cantrell there never was if I've ever seen one. Son, you need to feel to function, so it's time. Let's do something about finding the girl. Don't leave it to others." Paul finished with a hint of tears in his eyes.

After studying his grandfather awhile, Rhys realized what the old man was trying to do. "Thank you, Grandfather."

Rhys stood, shook hands with his grandfather, and then left the room. It was time to do what needed to be done. Time and effort, lots of dead ends, false leads that went nowhere to this day — all of it, which lead to the present day, five years after Bree went missing, when they found her sitting in their own backyard, at Sam's Place.

CHAPTER 8

"RHYS." NO ANSWER. "RHYS!" ETHAN tried again. "We're almost to the airport."

"Fine, is the plane ready to leave?"

"The arrangements were all made while waiting at Alan's. The pilot is there, we'll leave as soon as preflight is completed."

The car stopped. Rhys reached up across the seat and laid his hand on Craig's arm. "I'm depending on you and dad to hold things together here. We'll see you soon, no doubt."

Opening the car door, Rhys lifted out the unconscious woman from the back and they walked to the plane. Entering, Rhys placed her on one of the seats, while Ethan went to inform the pilot it was time to leave when all was in order.

Rhys sighed as he sat across from his passenger; he was so tired. He now knew what it must feel like going through war, mentally. He fell asleep five minutes after take-off. Two hours later, the plane was touching down at the ranch's airstrip. Ethan knew it was time to wake his brother. "Rhys, time to get up."

Rhys sat up with a start. Maybe it had all been a nightmare. But looking across the short space between seats, there was his wayward wife. He guessed it was real enough. Sitting there staring at her, he thought, *Did I ever really see her for who she was?* His first thoughts had been along the lines of believing she was a goddess. Had he put her on a pedestal and left her there?

He heard her moaning. Was it time for another sedative, or was it too soon? No matter, he wasn't ready to deal with all the crap right now, so another pill it was.

One of the ranch hands was there with a car to take them up to the house. Rhys carried her upstairs to their old room. Putting her there made him feel as if he was drowning in emotions. Standing, looking, knowing that she had the same effect on him as before, wounded him to his core. The face was still angelic. Turning quickly, he left the room.

Later, Ethan found Rhys in the library with a half empty bottle of scotch. "I don't think it's going to help your situation, you do realize that."

Rhys sighed, feeling dejected. "Probably not, but I need it so I can't feel for a time." Pouring another glass, Rhys still couldn't quiet his mind. When another hour passed, Rhys knew it was time to go to bed, and stumbling upstairs, he entered his room. Leaving a trail of clothes across the floor, Rhys dropped onto the bed. His feet had carried him there automatically, and when he fell into bed, his shoulder touching his wife's, he was too tired and tipsy to realize that he should probably sleep elsewhere. So, for the first time in five long, lonely years, he would be sleeping with his wife.

Just before dawn, Rhys woke to find a warm body snuggled against him. Lying there, he was trying to remember every part of her. Having had enough with memories, he began letting his hands familiarize themselves with said body. He had need of those lips after being denied their taste of honey for so long. He started to kiss her, and it seemed as though there was something different about it, as if the honey had a sweeter taste than he remembered.

Deepening the kiss, she was returning it with equal fervor. The passion was taking over like it always had. His wife was moaning and moving against him, and Rhys let himself go with it. Lost in the passion, he positioned himself over her saying, "Bree, I'm sorry. I can't wait."

Rhys sank home, but she cried out in pain. She stiffened and tried to get away from it all. Rhys was caught by surprise for a moment. Had she tightened up that much after having a baby? Trying to soothe her, Rhys said, "Shush sweetheart, be still. I know I startled you, but I need you now."

Riding the crest of a rainbow, Rhys was crying out. "Bree, Bree." It had never been this intense, so why was it now? But he didn't really care at the moment. After fifteen minutes of being tied to each other, all hell was about to break loose.

Catching Rhys off-guard, she rolled away from him the moment he removed himself from her. She shrieked at him, "You low-down bastard! Who do you think you are?"

Rhys pulled himself up short. She was backing towards the open window. Moving away from the window toward the door, she was thinking of leaving the room. "Come back to bed, Bree. Don't put us back through all the garbage."

Shaking her head no, crying, she shouted, "Whose Bree? And what have you done to me?" She was angry with this man for everything, but at herself for coming unglued. What was wrong with her? She shouldn't lose reason so quickly. It was time to leave this funny farm.

Leaping from the bed, Rhys pinned her to the wall in seconds. Instantly, she was pounding his chest, and squirming to get away from this maniac. Rhys took both of her arms in his hand then held them above her head. "Dammit, hold still. What the hell is wrong with you?" Rhys lifted her chin to look into her eyes for the first time. He was taken aback by what he saw: sky-blue eyes stared at him, not jade. It was a mistake, or the light was playing tricks on him.

Rhys shook his head. "You have blue eyes."

"Yeah, had them my whole life, about twenty-five years."

"That's not right, you're twenty-eight," Rhys said.

"Like I wouldn't know how old I am. Get real buddy. You need to get off of me, now."

Rhys kept looking at this person. How, why?

Had known that something had been different. How could there have been a mistake? What should he do now? So many questions were running through his mind. Still, he had no idea of who she was. She looked so much like his wife. What kind of monster did she take him for?

Damn.

He just took her virginity.

Double damn.

Rhys needed answers. "Who the hell are you?"

She was fed up with this whole thing. Getting her spunk back, she wasn't through fighting this person. Looking him right in the face, she suddenly spat at him. "GET OFF ME, you son-of-a-bitch!"

Rhys's temper spiked. No one had ever spit on him before, and he didn't particularly like it. Giving her a shake, he let her realize he was serious. "I'll ask you this only once more. Who are you?"

"I'm sure you really care!" She shouted, while glaring at him. "Would any woman have done for this side show, or was I chosen specifically? What's wrong with you? I was grabbed from the street, and dragged to God only knows where."

In a tone of voice that frightened her, Rhys said. "I told you I wouldn't ask again. Do you want to see what the consequences of defying me are?"

With her courage waning, there was a hint of tears. On quivering lips, she stammered. "Sky – Skylar Evans."

Rhys raised himself off her. Pulling clothes on, he said, "Get cleaned up. The bathroom is through that door. We'll talk after breakfast, and sort this out." Surveying the room one last time, his eyes stopped at the bed. Evidence was there for all the world to see: a small amount of blood on the sheets. Disgusted with himself, he left.

Skylar couldn't believe the nerve of the jerk. Like this was her fault. In a dazed state of mind, she asked herself what had happened here. Had he kidnapped her to rape her? Would he continue to do so? Would he sell her? Or was this really just some kind of sick mistake? Gathering up clothes, she went into the bathroom. A shower would help to straighten out her head. Not trusting the big jerk, as she didn't even know his name, it would be safer with the door locked so she slid the lock home.

With the door locked, and the hot water steaming the small room, Skylar could better assess the situation. She felt sore and sticky, and seeing a small trace of blood on her thighs made it all the more real. Skylar let out a blood-curdling scream, enraged at the injustice of it. Then, oblivion overtook her.

Ethan had been on his way upstairs to get changed for riding. Upon hearing the scream, he took the remaining stairs two at a time. Reaching Rhys's room, he threw open the door. Seeing nothing at first, he went across to the bathroom. Trying the knob, he found it locked. He pounded the door and called out her name, "Bree, open the door!"

No response.

"Bree! Dammit, answer me!"

Deciding he needed to remove the knob, he took out his pocketknife. He continued with the task at hand as quickly as possible.

Rhys walked towards the stables, which had been his thinking place when he was here with Bree before. What had he done? Guilt was plaguing him. He didn't relish meeting up with her again. Skylar. Her name was Skylar. He needed to remember her name.

In the end, he treated her like a whore, telling her to get cleaned up. She was probably in shock, and he just left her. The blame was all his; he was at fault. With the thought fresh in his mind, turning, he went back to the house. Rhys had to check and see if she was alright. She had said her name was Skylar. It was different, but it was nice.

Maybe he could try to explain it all to her, if she would listen. He wanted, no needed, for her to understand. Not finding Skylar downstairs, he headed for his room. Rhys found Ethan there, knife in hand. "Just what the hell do you think you're doing to the door?" Rhys shouted.

Ethan turned and looked at his brother. "I was on my way to change, she left out a scream like you would not believe, and I saw you just leave the house, so figured I'd better check and see what was wrong. She didn't answer. The door's locked. Taking off the knob seemed the right thing to do. Didn't think Gramps would want his door smashed. But hey, if you think you have a better idea, then by all means, do it yourself."

Rhys was furious with himself. "Don't be a smart ass. Finish getting the knob off." Horrors were running through his mind. Had she fallen? Maybe everything was too much and shock had set in. Could she have just lost it?

The screws were out, and pushing the door fully open, they saw her lying on the floor. Ethan saw a faint trace of blood on her thighs. "Oh my God," he said while shaking his head. He looked from Rhys to the girl. "She's not Bree, is she?"

His brother confirmed it. "No, she's not. Dammit, just get out of here. I'll take care of her myself."

Ethan didn't move; he was racked with guilt. Because of him, whoever this girl was, they had grabbed her and changed her life forever. How was it possible? He had put this girl in a position she didn't deserve! Never could he forgive himself for the hurt he had inadvertently brought to her.

Hearing voices brought Skylar around. She opened her eyes, and then slowly, she sat up. Who was with her? Why was she in a bathroom with two men? Things were making her uneasy; she inched backwards to the wall. Where was she? Who were these people? She wasn't focusing well. Her mind was hazy. One of them was reaching for her, and it all came crashing back into focus. She screamed and flinched away.

Rhys was feeling disgust for himself, so didn't sound sincere. "My word woman, I'm not about to jump you, you know."

Looking daggers at him, Skylar snapped, "How would I know your intentions? You jumped me before. What's to stop you now? Oh, just go away and leave me alone! I want to get cleaned up, without an audience."

Rhys didn't know how to proceed. He expected her to rant and rave, even cry. Not this one, though; she was spitting fire at him. Feeling somewhat helpless, and a little baffled, Rhys took a few deep breaths to calm himself. Talking in a low steady voice, he began, "Listen, I believed you were my wife. The disbelief in your eyes shows you probably won't want to believe anything I have to say. But please, let me at least try and tell you what happened."

All Skylar wanted was a shower. Couldn't they do this later, when she was clean and clothed?

Rhys slid down to sit on the floor with her. He knew where this story should start; it would help in explaining it all. "Ethan, would you grab the wedding photo. It's in the top drawer of the nightstand."

Ethan fetched the photo, and then passed it to the girl. "For what it's worth, I'm sorry. I was so sure. Damn me to hell!" Ethan left with a heavy heart. He was going to call Alan. He was positive help would be needed with this situation.

Rhys talked while Skylar studied the photo of Bree. "Until it was too late, I had no idea I was wrong. When the passion took over, I was gone. You want to call me a liar, and deny the passion was on both sides, but it was there, so there's no sense in lying to the both of us. There is no excusing what happened. I'll try not to let it happen again."

Skylar remained quiet, staring that the photo.

"Dammit, would you say something? Anything? If you could try to understand! Use your eyes! You see the picture. Tell me what the difference is. Scream, yell, or throw the damn picture at me. Just do *something*."

She sat there, not wanting to believe. It was freaking unbelievable.

"Dammit, my wife was missing for five years," Rhys murmured. "When I was told she was at Sam's, I leapt at the chance of seeing her. Finally, to be able to confront her! I would be able to ask her all the questions that I've had for years. The biggest being why she left me." Rhys was choked by emotions by this time.

"I thought you were her, that it was finally going to be over. I had found her. I never saw your eyes until afterwards. There I was looking into them, seeing blue instead of green." I felt you stiffen, but didn't have a clue as to why. I thought I imagined a barrier; you couldn't be a virgin."

Dropping his head to his knees, he continued. "But I messed up, didn't I?" What else could he say, or do, to make her understand?

Skylar had listened, but couldn't understand herself. She was feeling compassion for this man, due to everything he had gone through. She gave herself a mental shake – what was wrong with her? She had put up with so much. Pushing the photo across the floor, she stood and tried to speak. Only a squeak came out. "Ah –"

Swallowing, she tried again, "Could I be alone? I don't know what to think or feel at this point. I'd like to get cleaned up. It'll give me a little time to myself to think."

Rhys nodded, understanding. "We'll talk more when you're done up here. Just come to the library. We'll try to sort it out."

The utter gall of the man. It didn't sound like he was asking, but instead, giving orders again. And like she knew where the library was.

Fuming, she thought, *who does he think he is?* Shaking her head, she climbed into the shower. Her mind was wound tight.

A lot had happened: kidnapped right off the street, mind you, hit and knocked out, drugged, and brought to this place. And let's not forget, unwillingly ravished. But he *had* been able to arouse her to the point of abandonment. Was she an easy woman? She had had sex with a stranger, for goodness sake! What was wrong with her? She was beginning to feel helpless and close to tears again. The tears made Skylar angry with herself.

Well, damn both of them. She would show them. Being a helpless female was not in her make-up. She had lived, growing up, with Lainey and grew stronger because of it, so there was no sense changing now. With her mind made up, it was time to walk out of this nut house. Surely a town was close by that she could get to.

Did he think she would meekly go to him? No, that was not happening. Crying was not helping, so it was time to get her mad back on and show them. Did he blame her? It wasn't her fault she looked like his wife. The decision made, she headed for the stairs. Reaching the bottom, the front door was just there, and there is no time like the present to make an escape.

CHAPTER 9

LITTLE DID SKYLAR KNOW, RHYS had been staring out the window, waiting for her to appear. "Son-of-a-bitch!" Spinning around, he charged after her. Damn the woman! Didn't she have any sense at all? He knew he would have to fight her at every turn now.

Ethan had seen her, too. Jumping back on his horse, he turned and went after her.

Hearing the pounding of hooves coming hard behind her, Skylar decided it would be best to run like hell, and couldn't bother with looking back. She had only made it a few more yards when someone reached for her and pulled her easily on top of a horse. It was time to fight for her life, so wiggling and squirming, she caused both her captor and herself to slide off the horse. Upon hitting the ground, Skylar was stunned. It was hard to catch her breath, but got up quickly anyway. She turned to run before her life was changed even more, green and blue dancing before her eyes as her body fought to take in more oxygen.

Quickly looking around to see which direction to take, she couldn't help but feel overwhelmed and lost. She still couldn't catch her breath, but fear was tugging her onward. She picked a direction, and turning, she took a step. And came face to face with Rhys. Whirling around, Ethan was on his feet once more, blocking her path. Feeling like a trapped animal, Skylar was close to losing control. She began shouting. "Leave me alone! What's wrong with you people? Haven't you put me through enough?"

Breathing heavily, she continued. "You know I'm not this Bree person, yet you're stopping me from walking away. WHY?" A loud sob came out. "I just want to go home. Please leave me alone, and let me go."

Already feeling guilty, Ethan spoke calmly to her. "Listen, we're not going to hurt you. You can't walk away. The nearest town is fifty miles away ... and you were running in the wrong direction. Besides, you and Rhys have some talking to do about what happened between the two of you."

Both men were edging closer to her. Skylar's voice rose to a screaming point. "Stay – stay back! You don't understand anything. I won't be made to feel like a prisoner ever again!"

Where was the girl from upstairs? *She* had been spitting fire, but now, most likely, Skylar was going into shock. Rhys could see the fear clouding her eyes. They needed to get her help. Rhys knew if he pushed, the hysteria that was close to the surface would break through.

Skylar felt herself falling apart. Would she shatter into a million pieces? Wrapping her arms around herself, she told herself that she just needed to hold on for a bit more. Keep everything out, and away. She knew if she didn't calm down, the breaking point was too close to the surface.

Ethan stepped closer, but reaching out his hand caused Skylar to stiffen and try to lash out. "We want to understand. Let's talk, figure things out. Then we can get you what you want."

Skylar needed space, but they kept coming closer. Irrational thoughts crowded her mind. What was she thinking? Edging back, she was getting close to the pond's bank. Where did the pond come from? How had she not seen it before now? Maybe she should swim away. Could she make it? Not likely...so tired.

Minutes were ticking by, and finally, Skylar spoke in a shaky voice. "Every time ... my life ... was never to be my own. Why can't I ever be free? Something always steps in. Granny, mother, and now you people." Sobbing out loud, Skylar was trying to pace, but was unsteady on her feet. Rhys and Ethan had no idea what she was talking about. "Oh why? Why does this happen? I'm not a bad person." Her voice filled with emotion as she begged to know why.

Ethan once again tried to soothe her. "Look, my name's Ethan Cantrell and this is our Grandfather's ranch. You've kind of already met this other guy, my brother Rhys. Maybe we should go up to the house and sort things out for you. Let you rest, then let you call someone."

Rhys had remained silent, not because he didn't care, but because he hadn't wanted her to try and take off again. It was better that Ethan was talking, he wasn't the one who had hurt her. They all stood looking at one and other. Rhys was worried. Skylar was pacing close to the edge again. He could see the tension and hysteria in her. Then, suddenly, she tripped over a root and hit her head before either of the men could catch her. Rhys reached out his hand to help her, but she shied away, and crawled over to the base of the large maple tree.

Skylar pulled her knees up and began rocking to and fro, crying again. Rhys knew they had to get her up to the house. Her head was bleeding, and it was clear she was exhausted. She was rambling a story as she rocked, which had to be about her life.

Ethan had leaned down. "Skylar, let us take you back to the house. Your head's bleeding, in case you don't know it. You could lie down for a while, then see what you want to do. Let us help you."

Shaking, Skylar pulled back against the tree. Who was this person? Where was she? "No, who are you? Stay back, do you hear?" She was confused, and her head hurt. Raising her hand to rub her head, she brought it back down with blood on it. Shock was setting in once again. She was cold and her mind was foggy.

Rhys motioned for Ethan to back off – to leave her alone. Ethan knew not to question him any further. Turning, he grabbed the reigns of the horse. It was time to call Alan in.

Rhys knew if he tried to touch Skylar now, she would fight to her last breath. He didn't want her hurt any further. He needed to be patient – let her cry a little longer, try to get her to get up on her own. If not, it would have to be done the hard way.

It was only about five minutes though when Skylar quit crying. Rhys moved closer, only to see that exhaustion had taken over. Reaching over, he lifted her into his arms and headed to the house. Sleep would be the best thing for her now.

This was the first time, that as he looked into her face, he didn't see Bree.

So much pain in her life, and he had contributed to it. It felt right to have her in his arms. She would need to be held; he would have to help her put her world back into proper prospective. Could he be that someone? He felt sure that he would be a big part of her life now.

Alan was there when Rhys got to the house. With Rhys's help, Alan proceeded to check Skylar over. Determining that there was no other damage, he cleaned her head up and bandaged it. "She's going to have a hell of a headache."

Alan looked at his brother, sneaking a glance at the anxious man. Had he ever looked this unsure of himself? "She'll probably sleep the clock around. I was already on my way when Ethan called; Chelsea said to get my backside out and save you from yourself, before you did something you shouldn't." Alan grinned, but it quickly turned into a grimace. What had Rhys done to the poor girl?

"Ethan told me the highlights of what happened. Once she's rested, she will need answers that make sense. We should ask if there is any family to call. Having them near might make things easier for her."

Rhys remained silent as Alan continued to look at his brother.

"Talk to me Rhys."

Sitting by the bed, Rhys began talking. Two hours went by as he told his older brother everything.

Alan checked on Skylar again, and then motioned to the door. Rhys looked back at the sleeping girl as they walked out of the room.

Rhys headed for the library; he had a need to find out what he could. Some of those answers had to be in her purse. Pulling the bottom drawer open, Rhys lifted out her bag. *Do I, or don't I?* Women were funny about their purses. What the hell? He needed answers so he could help her. This could only do them both good. He dumped the contents on the desktop and rummaged through the mess that fell out.

The brothers walked in. They stood there sending Rhys questioning looks. Rhys looked back. "I have to find out what I can, anyway I can. Do either of you realize what we – no, correction – what I put her through? What I've done to this person?"

Nothing was said and the brothers decided to help. Going through every item in the purse, they couldn't help but question how all of this could have happened. She looked so much like Bree. If you didn't know any better, you would think they were twins. *Except for the eyes,* Rhys reminded himself, *those damn eyes.*

All they found were what all women carried, and her vital statistics.

Twenty-five, five-foot six, blue eyes, strawberry blonde hair, one-hundred and eighteen pounds. She had a reasonable bank account balance. Her cell phone had one number she called many times.

Rhys found a recommendation letter that a Mr. Blackwell had written for her. Seemed he was a former boss. He must have thought greatly of her by how the letter was worded. Should he call and ask about her?

What was he thinking? It was best to leave that for now. What would he say, anyway? That he had abducted Skylar because he believed her to be his missing wife? Besides, did he want anyone outside his own family to know what had occurred? Damn, his life was a bigger mess than ever before. What should he do now, with the woman named Skylar? Getting up, Rhys carried her cell to the window, stewing over whether or not he should make a call to the number used so often.

All was calm on the outside, so why couldn't it be calm on the inside? Turning, he put everything back in her bag; it would be up to her to make any calls. It wasn't his right to call her people.

It was possible she was already carrying his child. Somehow, the thought was pleasant to him. Imagining a child growing inside her caused him to think of Bree.

His family had suggested it was time to start proceedings to have Bree declared dead. Did he still want to find her? What were his chances? He had searched for five years to no avail, so why search more.

Could he get on with his life? No, he was still married. Yet, he wanted to know why he had met Skylar. Could there be a chance for a life with Skylar after everything that had happened in his life and between the two of them today? It was a little early to be thinking along those lines. He was thirty-six; he should have a family by now. What happened to his other baby? If he could declare Bree dead, he could marry Skylar and give their child a name. If there was a child. What would Skylar think? Would it be fair to put things into motion? Why was he even thinking this?

How much would she fight him over this? He was sure she would fight him – tooth and nail, no doubt.

Shaking his head, he knew he didn't have this right. He was thinking too far ahead, but he did want it though, and maybe he should try to get her to fall in love with him. After all, he felt halfway there himself. Which he didn't understand.

Alan saw how tired Rhys was. "It's on the late side. Let's all go get some sleep. Some of the answers will come if you're rested. I'm going to check on her before I retire. See you all in the morning."

Rhys knew Alan was right, so followed suit going up the stairs. Upon entering his room, he saw Alan frowning. "What's wrong?"

"She's starting to run a slight fever. Could she have been ill, before coming here?"

Rhys shook his head and shrugged his shoulders, not knowing one way or the other. "I don't have a clue."

Alan went on. "You know it could be everything drained her, and her mind and body is fighting back. We'll wait and see how it plays out." He rubbed his hand over his face – this had been one bitch of a long day.

With a catch in his voice, Rhys was leaning over her. "I'll be watching over her tonight. It's mostly my fault she's here. I know she will be all right, wait and see. She's a fighter like I've never seen before. You didn't see her with us."

She had to be all right; he couldn't stand any more guilt. Alan left, and Rhys got a chair to sit vigil for the night. If he had to, could he will her to get better, even if it meant she would fight with him some more? He would make her, even if he crawled into that bed to have her fight him in person. She could make him regret all the wrongs she had endured, if she wanted.

Chapter 10

Rhys, Alan, and Ethan were all unaware of what was about to take place in their father's office the following morning. As Brandon and Craig sat with a large desk between them, discussing business, Brandon's secretary paged. "Sir, there is a young man here that says he must speak to you, it's very important."

"Send him in, I can spare a few minutes."

When the young man entered he stuck out his hand to shake. "Sir I know you have no idea who I am, but my grandfather, Ben, worked on Mr. Paul's ranch for over twenty years before his accident. He told me I had to tell you the date of April 18th 2006, or close to it. He said those young people, Rhys and Ms. Bree, the happiness was back for them, it was in the eyes."

Brandon whistled. To be brought so abruptly into the world of five years ago was disconcerting and suspicious. "Who are you?"

"My name is Dave Jackson."

"And you say you're the grandson of one of Paul Sr.'s workers?"

Dave didn't exactly answer Brandon's question. He could see the pain and skepticism in Brandon's eyes and bearing. He needed to continue. "That morning, grandfather said he was cleaning out some shed behind the stables, when he heard someone by the door. He thought he was needed elsewhere, but heard someone talking.

"Grandfather could quote, word for word, what was said. I quote: 'I'll just have to get rid of her. If I can't get her away from that spoiled bastard, then no one will have her. It should be my baby she's carrying, not his.' Unquote."

Dave paused, waiting to discern Brandon's reaction, as well as Craig's. Both men's faces remained impassive, but he thought he saw some interest spark in Craig's eyes, and so, he carried on with his story, picking up speed.

"Grandfather knew who they were talking about. Whoever it was, knew someone had heard what was said. He felt he should slip out the back way and find Mr. Paul. It was then, before he reached the door to confront the person, that he bumped into something. The noise alerted the man in the next room, and he was attacked before he could leave the shed.

"Grandfather died last week, still trying to remember whose voice he heard. He said he knew the voice, but couldn't put a face to it."

Brandon and Craig sat listening intently to the story this young man was telling. Neither wanted to believe what they were hearing. Brandon sighed. "Are you positive about this, son?" After everything that had happened, he couldn't fully trust the young man before him, but he seemed genuine.

"Sir, I know you're probably thinking that I just want to gain something from this. Right? Well I'm going to tell you, my grandfather made me swear to come to your family about this. With his dying breath, he asked this of me. This is the last thing I can do for him. When I give my word, I keep it. I don't want anything in return.

"To have him remember, and believe he could help find Ms. Bree, was enough to give him some peace. His heart had been so heavy, with not being able to help. Two years ago, he wasn't satisfied with the police work and he wanted the blanks filled in. He tried to remember, but he died with an easier mind than he has had for years because I agreed to tell you his story."

After all this time, for someone to come forward with information, right on the heels of Rhys finding Bree, it was a little too coincidental for him. "Would you repeat your story? Don't leave anything out." He needed to know everything and to fish out the answers for himself.

Nodding his head, Dave recounted the story again. When he finished the second time, something hit him. "Damn! I almost forgot."

Brandon and Craig still looked unsure, but Dave knew why. He had forgotten a key piece of information that would solidify his connection, as well as his grandfather's, to the Cantrell family, and more specifically, to Paul Sr.'s ranch.

Looking towards Craig, he continued. "I imagine you remember Grandfather quite well, because of the time he had to tan all your hides. Ben told me I must remind you, so you would know he had his memory still. I can't believe I forgot to tell you."

Brandon and Craig looked at each other, and exchanged knowing glances. "We understand what he meant. We knew there was something missing from your story. We can't take the word of everyone who comes in. Ben knew what it would take to make us sit up and take notice. We have to be sure, and since telling us that last part, we are."

"I'm sorry it couldn't be more." Sighing, the young man stood to go. "I gave my word to tell you. I've done what I promised. I've got a clear conscience."

Craig shook the man's hand. "It's more than we've had, so don't feel bad. And I do remember Ben. He was a good man. We're all sorry he was caught up in it back then. He was hurt real bad, but we're glad he survived, and lived to give us these clues. Ben was always a good man...right to the end."

Brandon got up from the desk to show Dave out, and then began pacing back and forth; he was thinking of those days, five years ago, trying to recall what had taken place. "I remember Ben had been missing for about two days, before he was found. One of the hands was riding up on the north ridge checking out the fence line, when he came upon Ben. We were sure he was going to die, but he didn't.

"He couldn't remember any of us when he came to, let alone what happened to himself. Bree had gone missing the day after he had. So, more or less, we put Ben to the back of our minds. Our concentration was on finding her.

"What happened back then? Do you think Bree is telling them any of this? If someone was after her, how did she get away and stay hidden for so many years? Damn, could they have let Ben overhear, just to lead us in the wrong direction when asked? When he got hit, he was hurt far worse than they probably planned."

Craig remained silent, letting his uncle talk and sort through all of the information he had.

Brandon knew what had to be done. "Craig, I think you better get out to the ranch with the rest of the boys. Tell them everything. Ask questions. Get out the old records and check for anything out of place. You know what to look for – others have tried to hide things from us and it always comes out in the end to bite them in the ass.

"I'll give the boys a call, tell them you're on your way. Put them in the picture, till you get there and tell the whole story. Let's not leave anything unturned this time. I mean *anything*. Even if they got Bree to talk, we don't know if she will tell the truth to Rhys. Or maybe she won't remember what took place. And I for one would like to know what happened."

Craig left while Brandon was punching in the number for the ranch. After talking to Rhys, he was uneasy. Something was wrong.

Craig arrived at the ranch around two in the afternoon. He was met on the porch by the family, evidently waiting impatiently for him to arrive. But not for the reasons Craig thought.

"We'll talk in the library." They all filed into the house. Rhys spoke before Craig could start. "She's not Bree. I found out when I looked into her eyes the first time. Her eyes are blue, not green. Besides, she's only twenty-five. The rest doesn't matter right now." Rhys didn't want another person's disgust on top of his own.

Craig couldn't believe it. She wasn't Bree. But he saw her, and if she wasn't Bree, then who the hell could she be? They say everyone has a twin in the world, but this was uncanny. He retold Ben's story, letting them know everything he knew.

Then it hit him. "Could Matt be trying to pull something again?"

Rhys's blood was boiling; he didn't want to think Matt would be behind this. "No, I don't think. He would have been calling about now if it was his plan. Besides, he changed after Bree went missing. He wanted to be part of our lives and our child's life. So I have to say no."

Rhys paced, running his fingers through his hair. "What if someone on the ranch really did do Bree harm? What if he's still here? Dammit, if this is true, then Skylar could be in danger just by being here!" He could only blame himself, but he didn't like that tactic, so he said, "We need answers and a plan. The whole ranch knows I brought her back here. I believed she was my wife, and they will, too. If we're mistaken, then someone else could be, too. I won't have it happen again. If everyone else thinks Skylar is Bree, then maybe, just maybe, we can figure out who harmed Bree five years ago."

Ethan looked at his brother. "Maybe we could get Skylar to help us? If whoever did this to her is still here, they'll want to protect themselves. She looks so much like Bree. She could easily pretend to be her, but without her memory. Having her here will certainly raise tensions. Someone's bound to make a mistake by talking to her, or doing something else."

Rhys was jacked. "Dammit! Don't you think she has had enough to deal with due to me? I won't ask anything more of her! We need to get her out of here to safety. Besides, why would she even consider helping? I hurt her, badly. No, I forbid anyone from saying a thing to her about this. Do you all understand?"

Not one of the four were prepared when Skylar spoke. It seemed she had been hiding in plain sight. "Don't you think I should be the judge of that?"

Startled, they all whirled to face her. No one knew she had been on the sofa, and had heard all they were talking about. Anyone could have been in there, listening.

Glaring at her, the anger was flying out of Rhys's eyes. "You shouldn't be out of bed!"

Using all the sweetness that she could inject into her voice, she smiled and said, "Oh really? But I'm so much better. Of course, I would say it was a good thing I got tired of those four walls upstairs. I only came down to read for a while. Now though, I'm glad I didn't stay in bed. Or take a book back up with me. If I had, would any of you gentlemen have told me this story? I think not."

They couldn't believe this girl; here she was, giving them something of a dressing down. She acted as if they were longtime friends. How could she act like this today, when only yesterday, they thought she would have a breakdown over it all? Apparently, she was much stronger than she appeared.

A little of the anger she was feeling entered her voice. "So, like the Four Musketeers, you think you have to protect little ole me, the fair maiden. Well, I have news for you, gentlemen. BACK OFF! I've taken care of myself my whole life, and I don't need any of you playing the knight for me."

Rounding on her, Rhys enunciated each of his words. "Shut … Up … Skylar," his temper rising with each word. "You have no idea, no idea whatsoever, what we could be dealing with."

Thinking there was too much tension in the room, Craig thought of a way to ease it. Looking to each man, then shaking his head, he threw it back and burst out in laughter. This act got all their attentions. "I don't bloody believe …." The others joined in the laughter reluctantly, they knew what was being referred too.

Rhys had a scowl on his face. "I didn't tell her." Looking at his brother, he saw the disbelief and laughter on their faces. "Well, I didn't tell her."

Thinking it would help if she got him off the hook, Skylar said. "Really, he didn't tell me. Not sure what it means. It's just that the four of you reminded me of them just now." Then, holding up the book she had been reading, they all erupted into laughter once again. The book was *The Three Musketeers* by Alexandre Dumas.

"Seriously though, I want to help after hearing the whole story," Skylar urged. "All of you were convinced I was Bree. Admit it. Well, maybe we could work that and use it to our advantage?"

They knew she had them, because it was true. But Rhys didn't like the situation one bit. This slip of a girl was actually enjoying their discomfort. He knew he had to make her see things for what they really were.

Rhys spoke sarcastically. "Okay, so we made a mistake, so sue us. I would be the first to admit you're Bree's mirror image. But it's too dangerous. Someone was out to get her, and we have no idea who. They could still be around. And just for the sake of argument, look at what has already happened to you at my hands. I wanted revenge on Bree for leaving, and I took it out on you. No, I won't have it. I don't need one more thing to feel guilty about. Stop and think for God's sake. Use that head of yours for a change. Besides, I don't want your help. You remind me too much of Bree."

Skylar knew he was trying to make her angry, and well, it worked; she was livid. Getting off the sofa, she marched right up in front of

Rhys and started to shake her finger in his face. "You – you just stop right there, the great Mr. Cantrell," she spat out. I'll tell you right now, I lived most of my life in the middle of a war, one way or another with my mother. I had to grow up fast in the real world, not this nice world like you did. Don't presume to tell me what danger is. I could tell *you* some stories."

Stepping back, Skylar drew in a shaky breath. This man had to see reason, and so she couldn't make him angrier. She had to be careful. "Listen, I learned to read people, growing up with the mother from hell. I had to or I wouldn't have made it. If I hadn't learned, do you think I could have pulled myself back after this kidnapping quite so easily? I admit I will have to work through some of it a bit more, but I've trained myself to let go and move on."

They were all staring at her; she was telling Rhys off. Not many people ever tried, because they wouldn't be able to get away with it. One of his looks usually stopped them in their tracks, but they weren't stopping this girl. She thought she heard someone say, "You go girl," but the voice was so low she may have imagined it.

Skylar thought she better continue. "I've gotten to know you by listening to you talk to each other. The emotions you have for each other are tangible. I believe you are honest, trustworthy men for the most part. The movies would have called this a comedy of errors. I'm not downplaying what happened, but we need to move on to the real problems."

She searched the faces around the room, and then pointedly turned to one face in particular.

"Rhys, you spent five years searching. You didn't give up, you kept at it. You think your motive was revenge. I think you needed to finish with it. You never turned your back, and it shows me what kind of man you are. It was a mistake." She was blushing beet red.

They were all too serious, which made Skylar believe the mood needed to be lightened. "After all, didn't I recognize all of you earlier?"

The men all looked at her blankly, not understanding. What did she mean? "Well, it isn't everyday a girl gets to meet the Four Musketeers, and live to tell about it, now is it?" There were chuckles all around, all but Rhys.

He didn't like the idea of her being in danger. What if the person was still part of the ranch? That meant whoever had hurt Ben, and most likely Bree, already knew she was back, or at least believed it was Bree, even though it wasn't. Damn he felt cornered. But he would not accept Skylar's proposal. To keep her safe, they would do things his way, or not at all.

"First, we finish looking over the ranch records to see who left or who was part time. Since Dad called, we've found nothing. We need to look for clues."

Ethan wanted to finish what he was trying to say earlier. "Rhys, this could work to our advantage. If it is a ranch hand, they believe she's here. If not, we let everyone know you've been reunited with your wife finally. We need to keep our eyes open more than usual. Naturally, this has to stay in this room. No one else must know."

Skylar thought of the Blackwells. They would be worrying since she hadn't called for a few days. "I need to call my family first. Tell them I'm going to be out of touch."

Rhys knew it was inevitable, but didn't have to like it. "It might work, but there are problems with your plan.

"One. What if it was a drifter or someone that was visiting at the time? Sure, Ben heard someone, but it might have had nothing to do with Bree. This would be for nothing, and I'm no closer in my search.

"Two. We can't be with her every minute of every day. If we are here, we have to help out. This is a working ranch. She will be alone here at the house with us out working. What then? She'll be completely vulnerable.

"Three. What about her eyes?

"And four, the biggest. She doesn't know anyone here. For God's sake, she doesn't even know her way around the damn house. We have a lot of work ahead if we want to make this plan work."

Sighing, Skylar approached Rhys. "You brought up some good points, but stop and think. They're not insurmountable. There are five intelligent people in this room. Surely we can try to find solutions for the problems. Sure, something unexpected could pop up, but we will deal with it when it does."

All sat brainstorming. Could they cover most of the bases?

Skylar turned. "I think I've solved a few of the questions. I normally wear glasses, so I could get colored contacts. My eyes would match Bree's, and no one would be able to question, based on that, whether or not she's really back. We can also invent a backstory. We can explain I had an accident five years ago. Amnesia covers a lot, like the biggest obstacles: not knowing my way around the house or the ranch, not remembering the workers, etc. If there was a drifter wouldn't it help with the cover story? He found me wondering on the road back then, and I've been wondering from town to town all this time. And, if this has nothing to do with Bree, she really just up and left, then I've had a vacation, if nothing else."

Glaring, Rhys snapped. "You think you have an answer for everything. What will you do if one of us slips? I mean like use your real name? Then what? As far as this goes, your name can't and won't be mentioned again, no matter what. For all intents and purposes you will become Bree, not just in name, but in actions as well. We tell none outside this room.

"You would be my wife. What about the sleeping arrangements?"

Skylar's face screwed up in dislike.

Rhys smirked, believing he'd won. "I see by your face, you didn't think ahead. You have to be believable, including down to the housekeeper. Skylar Evans will cease to exist. It will be as if she was never born. No contacting your friends again. Never referring to your past. You will take on Bree's past, present, and future. It will be as if you never were. Is *that* clear enough for you?"

"I understand. It's going to be hard, but we can do this. Maybe this could enrich my life somehow, you never know." Skylar sighed.

Rhys's head snapped up. "Answer me this, why do you want to help? My family and I are nothing to you. Besides, I would think you would hate our guts. Why not let me suffer a few more years of not knowing where Bree is, or what happened? What, you think you're in for a payoff? So how much?"

Shocked rebounded throughout the room. Alan was first to speak. "Rhys, you're a damn fool. How could you even ask?"

With sadness in her eyes, Skylar gazed at him. "Oh Rhys, don't be an ass. I don't want to gain some monetary prize. I've been helping people one way or another my whole life. What's one more, here or there? I've listened, and gained some knowledge of your family."

Skylar breathed a frustrated sigh, and then decided to tell all. She was scared, and Rhys had to know it. "I don't have it in me to hate, even if I tried. The only thing I hate is you thinking I would help for financial gain. There is another reason I want to help. I mentioned it earlier. What if someone else saw me and would think the same way you guys did? You know what I mean, make the same mistake in thinking I am Bree? Should I have to keep watching over my shoulder, and wonder if someone is out there? Just waiting, and watching, for a chance to harm me? I don't want to live in constant fear, so you think about that. This plan could help you protect me." Skylar turned from the men.

Rhys felt defeated. He had never thought that he might be putting her in even more danger if he let her go. "Fine, do it your way. But if you get hurt, it will be on your own head, not mine. Don't think it's going to be a picnic." So saying, Rhys slammed the door behind himself as he stormed from the room.

★★★

Two weeks went by, and still they were no closer to finding answers. The records had shown absolutely nothing. Patience was at an all-time low, as well as morale – they were all waiting for something to happen.

Skylar was perhaps the most at peace with the arrangements. She felt at home on the ranch, with this family. It was going to be hard when she returned to the real world.

Some of the ranch hands didn't know what to think of this new Bree. They were all told she had amnesia. She wondered to the stables on a daily bases, talking to the different ranch hands to see what she was like before. She told them she was sorry if she did or said anything to them that hurt their feelings. They began to relax around her and encouraged the visits.

She spent some time with Sarah in the kitchen asking how she made some of the dishes she served them for their meals. It was as though she fit right into life here now.

Rhys and Skylar spent a great deal of time talking and getting to know each other. Getting to know the real man was helping Skylar deal with everything that had occurred up to this point. Then it hit her – it almost seemed too easy. How had she fallen in love with Rhys, a married man? Is that what happened to her mother? Did she fall in love with a married man as well? Was Skylar just as bad?

CHAPTER 11

IN ANOTHER PART OF THE state, Paul Sr. was visiting his grandson, Jordan, and received a call. "Rhys found Bree, so let's head back to the ranch and check what's up."

If it was true, what would she be like after five years? Where had she been, and how had she disappeared? So many questions, so few answers.

Jordan glanced at his grandfather. "What the hell, she really turned up. We need to be there for Rhys. He is probably going to need help processing this and someone to help him keep a level head."

Paul sighed. "No truer words have been spoken."

They continued talking, trying to figure out how they could help when arriving at the ranch.

A Jeep had been left at the airstrip for them. The first person they saw when they pulled in was her. Leaping to the ground, Jordan reached out to embrace her. She stiffened at the contact, not knowing who the hell he was. "Bree, it is really you! When Grandfather got the call, we couldn't believe it. What happened, where have you been?"

Skylar could see the emotions on this guy's face, and knew the older guy was the Grandfather, but she still didn't know who they were. Stepping back, to put a little distance between them, she looked at them with questioning eyes. "Do I know you?'

Jordan's mouth almost fell to the ground.

Turning to the older man. "You must be Paul, Rhys's grandfather. You have a beautiful ranch. You don't have a clue, well most of the time neither do I. They tell me I have amnesia from the accident."

Was she doing the right thing, using the plan on his family? Would Rhys be angry if she lied to his grandfather? She felt nervous, unsure of in which direction to continue. "That's the reason Rhys brought me back here. Thought it might jar my memory. Alas, nothing as yet has surfaced.

"It's funny. At times I look at Rhys and think I don't know him. He said he's my husband, but I don't recall getting married. I realize I'm hurting him, but it's out of my control." Skylar shook her head, as if she had just noticed Jordan and Paul, Sr. "Why am I telling you all this out here in the drive? Honest, I'm not crazy."

"No, I don't think you're crazy." Jordan held out his hand. "By the way, my name is Jordan. I'm Rhys's cousin. Paul Jr. was my father. We spent time together while I was here back then. I was training to be a counselor, and I helped you and Rhys find some common ground."

Skylar felt that something was off, but shook Jordan's hand to be polite. Could Bree have been having an affair with this joker? With everything she had been learning about the woman, the possibility was there. "Maybe you could fill me in on things from before – the things you helped Rhys and me with?" Skylar asked before heading ahead of them into the house. "Let's go in the house, but you'll have to excuse me. I get tired very easy. So we'll talk later."

"Not at all. I can tell you look pale," Jordan replied. "Get some rest. We'll see you later." Jordan needed to find his cousin to see what his thoughts were. Why didn't Bree remember? Had Rhys found anything out?

Paul hadn't said anything. He knew this girl wasn't Bree. What the hell was going on? He noticed she was shorter, and around the eyes, something was different. Pulling out his phone, he rang Rhys, leaving a brief and terse message. "In the library, now."

Skylar was pacing. Should she find Rhys? No. She would wait until later. She hadn't lied to them. She *was* tired lately. She would stretch out on the bed for a while.

After meeting with his grandfather and being called out on not leveling with him, he knew his grandfather was right to do it. Rhys hurt, he had always been honest and up front with Paul. So he told him what had occurred since seeing her at Sam's Place. He also warned Paul that everyone must call her Bree, because you never knew who might be around to hear.

Rhys wanted to find Skylar. Entering their room, he found her asleep. She should always be in that bed. It seemed so right to him. With a wicked grin, he crossed the room. It was time to wake her with a kiss. Just like the fairytales his mother used to read them. Should he, or shouldn't he?

While he was deciding, Skylar put her arms around his neck and pulled his head down. The kiss was like coming home. Little did Rhys know, but Skylar had been dreaming this. Dreams had never been this good. They were lying in each other's arms, and then it hit Rhys just what was about to happen. He pulled back. He had given her his word.

Skylar jolted awake, embarrassed by her actions. What would he think of her? Looking through her lashes, she found him grinning. He knew what she was dreaming about. Damn him, how could he read her so easily? Maybe the floor would open up and swallow her. No one had ever died of embarrassment, but maybe she would be the first.

Shaking his head and grinning like a fool, Rhys murmured, "I was only going to wake you for dinner. But then —" Raising his eyebrows slightly he went on. "If you have something different in mind, I could forget my promise. Food will be there later."

Skylar bolted off the bed for the bathroom. "Are you an ass all the time or just with me?"

Rhys threw his head back in laughter as he was leaving the room. "See you downstairs then, sweetheart! By the way, I talked to Grandfather, too." Skylar didn't reply, and Rhys didn't know if she'd heard him.

Ten minutes later, Skylar was descending the stairs, thinking that two could play this game he liked to play. Joining them in the living room, she saw Rhys still had laughter in those eyes of his. When their eyes met, she missed a step, damn him. One look was all it took to fluster her. Should she play the tease and get him all hot and bothered? No, it would cause him discomfort, but she would suffer right along with him. She couldn't punish him, not without punishing herself. It was a two-edged sword.

After the meal, Rhys and Skylar decided to watch some TV. Skylar's eyes were heavy, and laying her head back, she fell asleep slowly, and while asleep, she slid to Rhys's shoulder. Both felt content, being side by side. It felt right. When the news was over, Rhys gently lifted Skylar, and went upstairs with her. Reaching up, she put her arms around his neck and snuggled in. It was good being carried in his arms.

Realizing where she was jerked Skylar out of sleep. "What the hell are you doing? Put me down right now!"

Rhys was too aware of Skylar at this point, so he stood her on her feet. Brushing his fingers down her cheek, he knew he should step back. Why did things have to be so messed up?

Why was she feeling anything for him, which was so wrong on so many levels?

Skylar was feeling unsure, and decided to broach the subject of his cousin. "Rhys, can we talk?"

Knowing what was coming, Rhys sat on the bed, leaning back against the headboard.

"What are you doing?" She asked.

With a gleam in his eyes, he replied, "Well I've learned in the short time I've known you, that 'let's talk' usually means the start of a long discussion. Figured I may as well get comfortable." Seeing her mouth on the verge of falling open, he patted the bed. "Come over here, sweetheart. I think it will be easier if we are close together. If you get stuck on what is happening, I could help." The gleam in his eyes turned into a wicked grin.

Glaring, she put her hands on her hips. "Oh, you're impossible. I want to talk to you, but don't want you angry. Can you listen with an open mind? For heaven's sake, get the shitty-ass grin off your face."

Rhys did his best to contain his mirth. Then, he patted the bed again, hoping to make her feel more comfortable and less on-guard.

Skylar told him about the initial meeting with Jordan and Paul and the impression the former left her with. "So, do you think they might have been having an affair? Rhys, did you hear what I said? Are you even listening?"

Rhys was stunned. This wasn't what he thought the talk was going to be about at all. Shaking his head, he thought back over what she'd just said. Jordan and Bree had spent a great deal of time together. But an affair? No. His cousin wouldn't cross that line, he was sure.

Straightening up, he asked, "What do you mean by thinking an affair was going on? Are you out of your ever-loving mind? We had been working on our problems. For heaven's sake, we were headed home! Besides, Jordan doesn't swing on that tree. I'm pretty sure he's gay."

Her mouth flew open. "Oh, well, how was I to know?" she asked incredulously. "I'm not the person he thought, so you tell me why I felt he was implying something?"

Rhys reached out and gathered Skylar into his arms, leaning his head against hers. "I don't know. I wouldn't think he meant anything, but he comes off in a weird way sometimes. The thing is, he helped us before." Skylar stiffened at the reference to Bree and Rhys being a couple.

"You know what I meant by us, don't make this harder. You don't need to be jealous of someone who is in the past. You're my world now, understand? The past is long gone."

"Why the hell would I be jealous?" Skylar said quietly, while getting off the bed. Things were getting out of her control.

Standing, Rhys reached out to pull Skylar into his arms once again. He didn't want to hear anymore talking. Kissing always shut her up. "Lady, you go to my head. Jordan must have meant he could help us again. Couldn't *be* anything else. He's all about his profession, okay?"

Skylar saw ghosts from his past come into his eyes. Pulling his head down and giving a kiss of comfort, she said, "Let's chase the past away. Let's hold each other tonight, and maybe we can both move on."

★★★

When morning came, Skylar was alone.

Rhys was in the library going over emails, and he opened the one from "Anderson's Feed Mill." Good, the feed he ordered was in. Closing the computer down, he decided to see if Jake the stable hand would go into town and pick it up.

When Rhys reached the stables, he didn't see anyone outside so headed in to see where Jake was. "Jake! Are you in here?" Rhys yelled.

"Back here boss, checking on Lady," Jake answered.

"Could you go into town and pick up the special feed I ordered? Stan Anderson sent an email saying it was in."

"Sure, I'll head out now. Nothing else pressing right now," Jake replied.

When Jake arrived at the feed mill, the owner, Stan Anderson, was talking to his son, Jeff, an off-duty state police officer, in transition to becoming an FBI agent. They all nodded to each other. Jake walked over to them. "Hi guys, here to pick up the feed Rhys had you order."

Stan shook his head. "Here I thought I would get a chance to see Rhys since he was down here. He usually is the one who comes in when he is at the ranch."

"I haven't seen him for awhile either," Jeff said.

Stan turned to his employee. "Go and grab that order for the Cantrells."

"Yes, sir," the employee answered reluctantly.

Stan turned back to Jake and asked, "So tell me why Rhys isn't here himself?"

The employee hurried to bring up a couple of the bags, because he wanted to hear what was going on. He'd heard some rumors that Bree was back, but that was impossible, wasn't it? So he found a nice spot, off to the side as though hiding, and was listening intently.

Jake had a huge grin on his face. "Well, let me tell you, Ms. Bree is back."

There were gasps all around.

"What the hell?" Jeff yelled.

"Why wasn't the FBI or our office notified of this – Rhys knows there is still an active investigation going on about her disappearance," Jeff stated.

"Quiet down there, Hoss. Go on Jake, tell us what is going on," Stan said.

Jeff sighed. "Dad, could we do away with the nickname! I am an adult now."

"Well, seems that they found her up there where they all live. But here is the kicker, she doesn't remember any of them or her life before. She's nothing like the bitch she was before. Remember how she used to treat us back then, Jeff? She even seems softer somehow. She comes down to the stables now and checks on the horses and such," Jake told them.

Jeff looked at his friend. "Jake, you need to tell Rhys we will be out to follow up. It has to be done. I'll contact one of my buddies at the FBI, they are going to need a statement for their files also. But tell Rhys I'm glad for him, too. I can't imagine what he's been through."

The employee was so engrossed in listening to the conversation that he had leaned into the shelving and knocked a can off the shelf.

Stan noticed and said, "What are you doing? How about you getting that order loaded into Jake's Jeep so he can head back?"

"Yes sir, just stopped to rest for a minute," the employee answered.

"How is he working out for you Stan?" Jake asked.

Stan shook his head. "I only hired him because of Sarah, being her nephew and all."

Jake shook his head. Some people were just good-for-nothings. "Put it on the ranch's tab. I'll tell Sarah."

The employee re-entered the store. "Mr. Anderson, I'm not feeling so well. Do you think I could go on home now?"

Stan thought he did look pale, and he had to rest earlier, so said, "Sure, let me know if you need tomorrow off, too."

The employee hurried and left. How was this possible? Was it really her? He had to find out. He had loved her back then. Could he sneak onto the ranch and see for himself if it was real? He had to try – he just had to.

★★★

•

Life was falling into a pattern. Skylar talked with Jordan, wanting to know the things he knew. She set time aside to visit the stables every day, to play with the kittens and to check on the horse, Lady. She would be foaling in the future. Paul promised it would be hers when it was born.

The stable hands enjoyed the visits, unlike before when she treated them all like second-hand citizens. She was nothing like she used to be. Now, she was full of questions about this or that. It surprised them, and it did their hearts good to see those two getting things back on track.

The ranch was a beehive of activity. The Fourth of July Barbecue had been arranged, and the ranch hands and their families looked forward to the event.

Still, nothing had been found to do with Bree. No ranch hands seemed uncomfortable that Bree was back. In fact, they seemed happy about it. Rhys was beginning to think she was just gone. The police had to be right; Bree had taken off for parts unknown and didn't want to be found.

Skylar seemed to feel differently. She was having one of her feelings – she knew something was coming and could sense red lights flashing. Going to Rhys about it, he shrugged it off as the anxiety surrounding the planning of the party. "Quit worrying, it's been four weeks and what has happened?"

While they were sitting on the porch, Jeff showed up in uniform, and wanted to see Bree himself and get statements for his office and the FBI.

Rhys looked at his friend and made an instant judgement call. "Let's go into the house so we can talk."

Jeff raised his eyebrows but followed Rhys and Skylar into the house. Once inside, they proceeded toward the library. Jeff shut the door behind them and pointed toward Skylar. "Okay – let's have the real story, because that sure as hell is not Bree. And before you try, let me point out that she is about an inch shorter and the small mole under her left eye is not there any longer."

"Dammit Hoss – you are *still* good." So Rhys told his friend the story.

"Let me get this straight, once you assaulted this woman, kidnapped her, and raped her, you then realized she wasn't actually your wife? Anything else you want to add?" Jeff couldn't believe this.

Skylar spoke up. "We need to calm down."

"There is no way I can file a report. Bree is not here and I won't lie. Rhys, you may have gone too far this time. If she wants to file a complaint, then your ass is toast," Jeff all but shouted.

Rhys sighed. "You don't think I already know this? She wants to help for some reason. And if I made the mistake by believing she's my wife, then she is in danger if the person is still around. They could make the same mistake, too."

"None of you know if Bree just left or something happened. You are putting me in a bad situation here." Jeff said with a little anger.

"Just give us a little more time. Could you come to the barbecue and be another set of eyes?" Rhys asked his friend. "If something is going to happen, it'll probably happen there."

Jeff felt he had to help his friend. "Fine. I'll be here, but then you will come clean to the office."

Jeff left, unsure if he was doing the right thing.

Skylar and Rhys looked at each other, not sure what should happen now.

Skylar was first to speak. "Well, I'm going – I mean I'll go and help Sarah with some of the planning of the barbecue.

Rhys nodded, then turned to look out the window and contemplate his thoughts on a deeper level. He wanted to talk with Skylar about the future. He wanted to make plans. Tonight would be the night; He was in love, and wanted a life with her. He would go and see the judge soon, and have Bree declared dead. Grandfather had said to get a special disposition. So, the final chapter could be wrote in the Bree saga. It was time to start a new one that included Skylar.

But, little did they know, the talk with Skylar would have to wait.

CHAPTER 12

Matt Landon arrived at the ranch after lunch. He was not a happy man. Someone had called to tell him his daughter had been found, and that she'd been staying at Paul's since the end of May. And not one of the family thought of calling him, mind you. Not one of the bastards had the decency to let him know.

He wondered who that had been on the phone. It most certainly wasn't one of the Cantrells, but that was no matter, at least he was let in on the good news. There was still going to be hell to pay for their silence; he had a right to know. After all, Bree was his daughter. Rhys of all people should have made him aware, and Matt was going to call them to the carpet for it.

Storming into the house, Matt was raging. "All right, were is my daughter? You people think you have the right to keep this from me? I should have been called immediately. Damn you all! Damn you to hell!"

Paul stepped out of the library. "Slow down, Matt. She is here, but there is a problem." He stopped there, unsure of how to proceed without Rhys here to back up the plan.

"Well, what's going on? I want to see my little girl!" Seeing Paul's face, Matt responded with apprehension. "Just spit it out Paul, don't whitewash it. Where is my daughter?"

"Rhys found her, but she isn't the same. Believe me Matt, no one decided against you knowing. It just happened that way."

"What do you mean she isn't the same?"

"Let's go into the library. You might want a drink and to sit down for this conversation. Paul motioned for Matt to take a seat, and then went over to get them both a drink. Paul retold the story, about Rhys bringing Bree to the ranch. He needed to pause to get his thoughts straight; he didn't want to say the wrong thing. "All right, you've heard most of the story. The biggest drawback, however, is that she has amnesia."

Matt couldn't take it in, but it would explain where she had been for the last five years. To have his daughter back, but no closer, he felt he was sinking in quicksand. Was Paul saying his daughter wouldn't recognize him?

Paul placed his hand on Matt's arm. "You need to get ahold of yourself before they get back from their ride. You do realize we can't just spring a father on her? She hasn't been told much about her life from before."

"I think I understand, but I don't like it. How will I hold myself back from her?" Matt asked with tears in his eyes.

"I think I can understand what you must be feeling. Give her a little time. In the long run, you'll see it will be worth it." Paul didn't know what else to say.

Matt rose to go to the door. "Do you think I could use a room? I need to think and rest a bit before dinner."

Paul heard the hurt in Matt's voice and nodded to him. He was afraid of how this was going to play out. He needed to send one of the boys out for Rhys, and called Ethan to go get him. Then, sending a text to Rhys, he typed, "Need to see you NOW. ASAP."

★★★

Being out all day in the beautiful weather is what they had both needed. Rhys felt his phone vibrate. He got it out and looked. "Guess we need to head back. Grandfather needs to see me."

Just then, Ethan came across them. "Granddad wants you."

"Yeah, just got the message." He said, holding up his phone. The three rode back to the house.

"Listen sweetheart, you go up. I'm going to stop and see Granddad, see what's up. I can join you in a few. If I hurry we can share – conserve water, you know." A roguish grin lit his face.

Laughter bubbled out of Skylar. "Rhys Cantrell, you get going right now. I think there is enough water for both of us to take our own showers. Besides, I'm starved."

"Starved, are you?"

"Oh *you*, for food. Maybe you later."

"Are you promising, my dear?"

"No, it's a threat."

"Good, I'll be right up then."

It didn't take Paul long to tell Rhys about Matt's arrival and the conversation they had had.

Rhys hadn't planned on his father-in-law finding out yet. This was a turn of events he didn't relish, but he went up to get ready for dinner. Should he clue Skylar in? No, let her continue to be happy for now. He also didn't want to cloud their story further. Knowing who the man was would make Skylar's part in the act of subterfuge all the more difficult. He did say, however, that there was an unexpected guest for dinner that night.

★★★

Hearing laughter in the hallway, the others in the room faced the door. It was good to hear happiness in the house again.

Rhys paused mid step, all the while keeping a close hold on Skylar, guiding her away from their unexpected guest. All he could hope, was that Paul's talk with Matt would help before the two met. Stopping by Alan, he left Skylar there to talk. "I'll be right back. I need to speak to our guest for a minute before I introduce you." Turning to Alan, he asked his brother to keep Skylar occupied. "Talk to her for a few, Alan, would you?"

Skylar noticed the stranger was already there. Who could it be? His back was to her, she couldn't get a look at his face.

Going across the room, Rhys held out his hand. "Hello Matt. I won't say it's good to see you. I imagine, or should I say, I *hope*, with Paul filling you in, it's enough for you right now just to be here. Understand?" The rest of the statement was left unsaid. Matt knew what was meant, and nodded slightly.

Going back over to Skylar, Rhys rubbed her shoulder gently. "Bree, there's someone here I know you're going to want to meet. If you'll excuse us, Alan?"

Rhys led her across the room. Why didn't the man turn around when he knew they were coming over? Bracing Skylar with his arm, Rhys started to speak, just as Matt turned to see his daughter. "Bree, this is Matt Landon, your father."

Matt was hoping for recognition, but was in for a shock. Skylar just got paler by the second. Her hand flew to cover her mouth, even as the scream was rising to her throat. She was unable to contain it. "No!"

A black abyss reached up to take her away. Everyone was stunned speechless. Rhys almost missed catching her as she fell. Why would she react that way? Why faint? What had startled her so? Rhys placed her on the sofa as Alan rushed over to check on her.

Rhys had to keep the pretense up, but was worried about his woman. "I don't understand. She has had no reaction to anyone else before. It was as if she was terrified by who she was seeing."

Emotional, Matt reached out. "Could seeing me have brought it all back to her? It could be too much all at once, don't you think?"

Rhys was damning himself. He should have told her who the guest was. But Matt couldn't be further from the truth. He was at a loss as to why this had happened. Alan was handed smelling salts to arouse Skylar.

Rhys leaned into Alan, and in a hushed voice, said, "Why? You and I know she never met Matt before this."

"I don't know. You'll need to get her alone and find out."

Rhys didn't like it. It had been a very real reaction to Matt, though. She wasn't playing at being Bree. What did Matt have to do with Skylar?

Alan got her to come around. She was blinking, trying to focus, and remember what had happened. Seeing the discomfort, Alan spoke gently, "Hey there. Are you alright, Bree?"

Skylar was shaky and somewhat frightened. Why now? This couldn't be happening. She looked around the room. "Wh – where's Rhys? I want to see Rhys."

Stepping around his brother, Rhys leaned down and took her hand, rubbing it to try and soothe her. "I'm right here baby, I'm right here." Gathering her into his arms, he wanted to comfort her. Skylar was clinging and sobbing, and it wasn't like her. After a few minutes, he knew she was calming down. She looked into his eyes, hoping she wouldn't need to speak. But she knew she would have to. "I – I want … I want to go upstairs. Please, Rhys."

Rhys knew she was honestly frightened, and standing with her, he proceeded to leave the room. Matt stepped in front of them, blocking their exit. "Bree, sweetheart. I'm your father."

Skylar didn't want to hear any of this. She wanted out of this room. Rhys tried to push past Matt to get her out into the hallway.

Matt didn't want to accept her wishes. "What's wrong? Talk to me. How can you be frightened of me? Answer me, Bree!"

Skylar buried her face in Rhys's neck, not wanting to face the man before her. Seeing this, Matt was infuriated. "Bree, I need some answers. Dammit! I deserve them."

Rhys had had enough. With a decisive look, he pushed past Matt. "*That* is *enough*. Shut up and stand back."

Matt stepped aside, feeling dejected.

After the couple left, Paul went over to Matt. "Matt, I tried to explain earlier, and you said you understood. She has had a lot of new people thrown at her in a short time. Rhys, first and foremost. You know how he is. Then coming back out to the ranch, and the boys are all here. She has to find out and learn about herself again, slowly.

"And then, if that wasn't enough to deal with, Jordan and I arrived. We are all strangers to her, and it's a lot for her to take in. Hell, it would be for anyone. She's been trying to connect the dots, but there hasn't been any luck. You're just one more person she should have known. You do have a point, though, and maybe it all came crashing back when she saw you. Give her some time and space to adjust.

"Talk with Jordan. He deals with this in his profession. It's going to be hard on both you and Bree, just as it's hard on all the rest of us." Walking away from the men, Paul wondered how he would feel if the roles were reversed. He had never been close to Bree; she didn't want to be part of his family. But this girl *was* family. He felt he needed to protect her.

Matt hadn't helped matters as he had wanted. Instead, he hindered them. He couldn't keep his emotions at bay, or his mouth shut. Had he made things worse?

CHAPTER 13

UPSTAIRS, RHYS WAS STILL HOLDING a sobbing Skylar. He had to get her to talk, find out what had happened, and why. Pulling back, he looked down at her, but this caused her to cry out in fright.

"Rhys, don't leave me. Please hold me a little longer. Please." A sob crept into her voice. "Please hold me."

"Sweetheart, I'm not going anywhere." Being this close was doing things to his sanity, though. He wanted to make love to her, but knew she was upset. He began to kiss her fears away. Both knew where it was headed, but neither cared. They were going to need their strength of mind to get through what was to come.

Laying there, holding on to one another, they wished their embrace would hold the outside world at bay. Rhys knew it couldn't last, though; he needed to know what had happened earlier, so they could deal with it.

"Baby, talk to me." He gently caressed her shoulder, coaxing her to speak. "Sweetheart, what happened downstairs? You weren't acting. It was if you saw a ghost. You were scared to death." Waiting, he was unsure if Skylar was going to answer.

Pulling away slightly, she looked up into his eyes. Taking a deep breath, she wondered how she was going to explain. "How could any of you just spring him on me?" She bit her lip. "Damn, it's coming out wrong. I don't know what to say, or how to put it into words. Dammit to hell, all I can tell you is I know him. I've seen his face before."

Rhys was smiling at her. Skylar was infuriated to no end. Seeing her anger, Rhys figured he had better explain why he was smiling. And he better be pretty damn fast about it. "Honey, I see fire in your eyes. Listen, before you fly off the handle. How could you help but not know the face? You see it every time you look in the mirror."

Not realizing the significance of his observations, Rhys shook his head and chuckled.

Someone was standing outside the bedroom, listening to the explanation closely. Being satisfied, they walked away quickly and quietly, not wanting to be seen. There would be no excuse to be in this part of the house.

It seemed as though Rhys was laughing at her. Did he think she was an idiot? With the fury barely controlled under the surface, Skylar gave Rhys a resounding slap across the face. Glaring, she got off the bed, turning to look at him. "How dare you! You couldn't begin to understand a damn thing I was telling you! It's not my face, as you casually pointed out. It's a face I've seen in a photo, time after time."

Rhys was stunned. Skylar threw open the closet, digging around in the back. She pulled her wallet out of her purse. Opening it, she pulled a photo out of a small slit in the back. Walking back across the room, she threw it at Rhys. Still shaking, she walked over to watch out the window, unsure what else to do in her angered state.

Reaching out, Rhys picked it up and unfolded the photo. His eyes bulged. He couldn't believe what he was seeing before him. But he also knew this photo had caused her so much pain. "I know the man has to be Matt. Unless he has a twin running around. Who the hell is the woman?"

"My mother."

"Son of a bitch. It means – "He couldn't say it, didn't want to think it.

"Remember, I told you about the picture – about finding it in my mother's things. When I saw it, I just knew he was my father. So I carried it with me because it showed both of them. I thought I might find him someday, just not like this.

"Coming face to face with him, I don't know. I think I felt like you guys did when you saw me the first time. It's like getting sucker punched in the stomach, quite by surprise. Too much was running through my head. I didn't cope very well."

The numbness was ebbing away, and now she was tired and worn out. Looking at Rhys, she was filled with remorse for hitting him. The print of her hand was evident. Going over, she reached out and gently touched his cheek. "I'm sorry. I lost control. Can you forgive me?"

"I'm sorry, too."

"Rhys, could I have some time to myself? Maybe an hour or so, then you can come back? I'm going to need you with me, after I get my head on straight."

He nodded. "Sure. I understand."

Rhys had his own thinking to do, and sleep looked like it was going to be impossible tonight. "I'll be back up in a while then."

★★★

He went in search of Alan, as his brother was a good and trusted sounding board. Too many emotions were coursing through him. He needed to talk about it all. After all, what was he feeling, with her looking like his long lost wife? Shaking his head, he realized they are half-sisters, three years apart. This was so messed up in so many ways.

How could he have fallen for the little sister now?

So much separated Bree and Skylar. Bree had all the advantages, while Skylar had to struggle for everything good in her life.

He knew now, that what he had felt before with Bree wasn't love, but mutual lust. With Skylar, though, it was all-consuming, involving not only his heart, but also his whole person. He was definitely in love with Skylar Evans. How did it happen so fast? He had heard about how his grandparents, and parents came together, fast and furious. Love at first sight; they had told the story many times. They say when it's right, it's right. Together they made a whole.

Was Skylar his whole? How did she feel about him? Were his plans for nothing, was it all an act. How much was she like her sister?

Rhys found Alan in the library, dozing in a chair. Giving him a nudge, Rhys woke him. "Can we talk?"

Yawning and stretching, Alan shook his head to clear it. "Sure we can. You know you never have to ask. What's up?"

Rhys told him everything he had learned, leaving nothing out. Then, when he was sure that Alan understood, Rhys asked his advice, something he rarely did. "What do you think I should do about Matt?

Is it fair to keep him out of the loop? There's something telling me to wait, see if anything else happens."

Alan took it in, before commenting. "I think you should wait. Don't go to Matt, yet. The least amount of people who know the true story, the better. I feel we've been missing something, too. Let's not jump the gun, so to speak. For some reason, I feel like Skylar could still be in danger. Whoever it was before, I think he's still around."

Rhys went to argue, but Alan held up a steadying hand to stop him.

"Nothing has happened, maybe nothing will. We don't know if this situation is solved or about to blow up. And we haven't been watching as closely as we probably should be. I don't know what to think about that."

"Come on Alan! If it was going to happen, why hasn't it happened already?" Rhys said.

"Call me an old lady, but I'm worried about this. Okay, point in fact, how did Matt find out?" Alan asked.

Rhys looked startled. "He said someone called him."

"That's right, but who was it? Think. It was someone on this ranch. No one else knows. What do you think?"

"I need to get to the bottom of this, and fast. We need to look at everyone who's here. Damn, look at the time. It's midnight!" Rhys yawned, it felt like it was time to get back upstairs and check on Skylar.

CHAPTER 14

Morning had Jeff driving out to the ranch. He wanted to be there early before people started arriving for the barbeque. He need to talk with Rhys more. When he arrived, the family was eating breakfast. "Morning all. Rhys can we go and talk?"

Paul looked at Jeff. "Sit down, son. At least have a cup of coffee with us."

Jeff took a breath. "Sir, this has to be taken care of before others arrive. But I will take the coffee with me."

Rhys and Skylar both rose to go with Jeff. At Jeff's look, Skylar said, "You are not leaving me out of this."

Both men were resigned she was joining them. When the door to the library shuts, Rhys turned to Jeff. "Well Hoss, what is it?"

"I need to stress this, when, not if, the bureau finds out she is impersonating your wife, this is going to raise more questions than you have answers for. I've known you my whole life and there is no way you did anything to Bree. But they don't know you."

Rhys stiffened. "Dammit, if I knew what happened or where she was – don't you think I would have gone after her, if for nothing else but my child?"

Jeff ran his hand through his hair. "Rhys, buddy, you are running up a tab you might not be able to pay when the time comes."

Skylar had listened to it all, then asked, "What should we do about this then?"

Jeff looked from one to the other. "That is a good question. Have everyone who knows what is going on listen and keep a close eye on everyone. I will roam around and watch, just in case."

Jeff pointed in Skylar's direction. "We need to watch the reactions of all toward her."

They all knew it was probably going to be a long day.

By lunchtime, everyone had arrived with their families. Skylar hadn't known what to expect. As she watched it unfold, what she was seeing was like a scene from the show, *Dallas,* which she had watched as a kid. People were playing horseshoes, volleyball, kids were running all around and some were just sitting and visiting with each other. Thinking back to that show, she laughed, something always happened during one of their barbeques. All at once, that sobered her up. Would something happen here, today?

Matt walked up to Skylar. "How are you doing? Anything I can do? I'd really like to spend more time with you today."

Skylar still felt she had to hold herself back. Something was off. What was giving her this feeling? "I'm fine, but I need to mingle with all the guests."

Matt continued to stay close to her, hovering, not letting her out of his sight.

Someone else was watching Skylar from the stables, believing she was Bree. All the while, he became angrier and angrier that she kept flittering around all those other men…the whore. Just like old times. But what scared him most, was the fact that she really did seem to be Bree. How could she be back?

Skylar had had enough of Matt's hanging around constantly, and she hissed quietly, "Matt, you need to give me some space. You are making me feel smothered."

Matt responded. "I'm just afraid you will disappear again. Am I so wrong to worry?"

Just as Skylar was going to respond, Jordan walked up. "Hey guys, can I steal Bree away for a minute? I have a couple things to ask her."

He steered her off to the side, away from everyone.

Jordan looked at her and could tell she just wanted to scream. "What's up? You seem unusually stressed as you talked with your father. Let's go for a walk down to the pond and talk."

Skylar was unsure; she still couldn't get a read on Jordan. There was just something about him. "No, but thanks for getting me away from Matt. He needs to back off some. I'm still just getting to know everyone, and I wish he could understand. I have no memories of any of you."

Jordan stared at her for a couple of moments. "Offer still stands for that walk, maybe later?" He gave her a smile and then walked away.

As the day was winding down, Skylar wet up to Paul. "It looks like everyone had a good time."

"Yeah, I think they did, honey." Paul answered.

Skylar hesitated. "Do you know where Rhys is? I wanted to speak to him but every time I go in his direction he's not there when I get there."

"Jeff had talked to each of the boys, so him and Rhys went inside to hash things out. Rhys is upset. He believed they would see or hear something, anything today. Kind of a letdown for him, not that we want anything to happen to you," Paul added.

Skylar was a little angry. "Oh, why didn't they get me to go in too?"

Paul heard the anger. "Dear it's not you. He was and is as close to Jeff as he is with his brothers. He just needs his friend right now, and maybe some distance will help him clear his head."

Skylar walked off. She felt totally left out. Why couldn't they understand she needed to know what was going on, too? It seemed that since Rhys found out who she was, he was avoiding her. Where had he been sleeping? He certainly wasn't sleeping with her. The bedroom seemed empty and lonely.

There are so many questions, but not enough answers. Skylar felt like she was going to go crazy. Should she just chuck it all? Would it bother him if she left? By ignoring her this last few days, Skylar was beginning to question if she had really started to get to know Rhys at all. Was it all an illusion for the sake of the others? Was she a fool, to dream a man like Rhys could like her? How did this happen so fast? Why did she even want to be with him?

Her mind continued to throw up question after question.

Her own mother had hated her, so was she destined to be disappointed in love, always? The Blackwells were the only people who had shown her love in her life. Should she have listened to Harry and stayed with them?

★★★

The next morning found Skylar still pondering what she should do. It hit her then that her period was a week late. Could she be pregnant? Hugging the knowledge to herself, she knew, that no matter what, she would have a part of Rhys to love in the years to come, even if he didn't love her in return.

One thing was for certain, Skylar was not her mother, and would never be like her. Her child would know love was present every day. Skylar would love her child above all, and not turn her back on it. No wonder she had been so tired lately. Maybe a little irritable, also, and weak. She had been taking it out on everyone, and now found, if she was pregnant, that she had some forgiveness to ask for.

Skylar knew if she told Rhys, it would change everything. He could get his divorce on grounds of desertion, or he could have Bree declared dead. Did she want him just because she was carrying their child? Likewise, if he knew about the pregnancy, would he want her only for the baby? No, if he didn't want her for herself, then he wouldn't have her, not at all. She wasn't about to marry for anything but love. She could go home and raise her child. But that wouldn't be fair to the child or Rhys.

It was time to find out why Rhys had backed off.

Meanwhile, Rhys was going through every file on the ranch he could find, and he was wiped out. He had to find something; he wouldn't stop, not until Skylar was safe. What were they missing? Who was around back then? Had anyone caused trouble? He felt like it was right under their noses. He had slept on the couch for so long his neck and back were killing him. The only rest he got was with her by his side. It would be his fault if something happened. That was the only thought that kept him searching.

CHAPTER 15

SKYLAR FELT WIPED OUT, THE heat was draining what little energy she had. She was going to sit on the porch swing quietly for awhile.

Alan was talking to his wife on the phone when he saw Skylar sit on the porch. He missed his wife and kids, but felt a duty to support Skylar. Going out onto the porch, he found Skylar had fallen asleep. "Bree," he said, giving her a gentle shake. "Bree, are you alright?" It was hard to continually call her by that name, but you never know who might be listening.

When she looked up, he knew she was pregnant. He was like his grandfather, being able to see it in the eyes. Why hadn't he thought about it before? No wonder she had been snapping at the littlest things.

"Yes, I'm alright. Just a little tired, I guess. I haven't been sleeping very well."

Alan wondered if she realized it yet.

"There's been a lot to take in. I'm going to go up and stretch out on the bed." Pausing, she looked back at Alan, with anticipation. "If Lady should start foaling, come get me. Please."

Paul was coming up the steps and overheard Skylar's request. He nodded, a grin appearing on his face. "I'll make damn sure to get you." He had noticed the look, as he called it, earlier today. He was having another great grandchild. That's what those two need, a bond lasting a lifetime.

Alan turned to his grandfather once Skylar had gone into the house and was out of hearing. "You know, don't you?"

"What do you think, son? I knew each time with your grandma, and mother. I hoped you would get this from me, you being a doctor and all. You take after me, at least in something."

Rising to his feet, nodding to his grandfather, Alan felt it was time to search out his brother, and talk with him about spending too much time in the library.

Alan didn't have to go far, however. Rhys had decided it was time to join in on dinner, and was in the hall. "Where's my wife?"

"If you cared, you would know. She's lying down, not feeling well. Lately, you have holed yourself up in the library. You need to spend time with her, not neglect her."

"Dammit, I've been busting my ass looking for a needle in the haystack! Besides I've had a lot on my mind." And it was true. Rhys was working hard to discover a link to Bree and her disappearance five years ago. He just refused to accept that she had left him willingly. Things were getting better, she was having his child, and they were soon leaving for home. No, she hadn't left willingly, something malevolent had happened to her.

"Your mind better damn well be cleared now." Paul had entered the house behind Alan, and he was surprised to see his grandson outside the library.

"Grandfather, enough!" Rhys was tired of everyone telling him what to do and telling him how he should feel.

"Don't you grandfather me, she needs you."

Rhys sighed. "I know. Things will get better, I promise."

Paul thought he should change the subject, so asked about Lady. "Rhys, do you think Lady is close to foaling? I gave the foal away already."

"What do you mean, you gave the foal away. Dammit, Bree is waiting for it."

"Calm down, fool. I gave it to your wife. I haven't kept a close eye, so I want to know."

Rhys was calmer. "Probably be a day or two yet before she drops it." His mind was elsewhere, thinking of the girl upstairs. He needed to be with her, since research wasn't getting anywhere. What must she think of him, not being with her for days?

Fear had kept him from going to her. Learning she was Bree's sister was only the tip of the iceberg. Or so he had thought, but Grandfather put a different light on things. He had a way of making you see things without saying much. But Rhys would make it up to her. Their talk was long overdue. It was six o'clock, so she should be ready to get up. He found her still sleeping; should he wake her or let her sleep longer? The latter was the best choice, so went back down to join the family.

Alan was on the phone with his wife. "Give Chelsea my love, brother dear."

Hanging up, Alan turned to Rhys. "You wait, one day you'll act the same. I'll lay money on it. They'll be here for the weekend. One more day of sleeping alone. I think I'll let the kids have you, for at least an hour," Alan laughed.

Grinning, Rhys shook his head. "A happy family man, I'll be there soon. Very soon if I have anything to do with it. Well big brother, how about a game of chess? Since you said I shouldn't wake her, it's only fair you entertain me."

"Sure, why not? As long as you don't mind losing, why should I care?" Alan quipped.

"You only wish, big brother. You forget, Grandfather taught me all he knew, while you were out playing doctor, with Sarah's daughter." Rhys chuckled.

"I was just starting my practice early, not waiting till I was too old to see what was there."

"You're crazy, big brother. Good thing Chelsea isn't the jealous type."

★★★

John decided to talk to his aunt, to see what was really going on out there at the ranch. He'd had enough with silent snooping – no more eavesdropping in the feed store or staking out in the barns.

He got a ride out with someone going close to the ranch. When he finally got there, he knocked on the back door, waiting for Sarah to answer.

"Look who's here," Sarah said while opening the door. There was a hint of a smile, but there were even more emotions that flittered across her face when she saw him.

"Hi, Aunt Sarah." John said.

"John, you know you shouldn't be out here. Mr. Paul done told you, you weren't welcome anymore," Sarah said sadly. "And I know you are working for Mr. Anderson."

"It's just been so long since I saw you," John said quietly and continued. He had to play his cards right, and Sarah was the easiest to use. "I got help for my problems. I'm doing much better. I heard Bree was back and wanted to tell her I still love her for helping all those years ago."

Just then, Jordan walked into the kitchen. "What the hell are you doing out here?"

"I missed my Aunt. Sorry, I'm going. I have things to do anyway. See you, Aunt Sarah," John said with a slight grin.

"Mr. Jordan, please," Sarah said. "How are you going to get back to town?" Sarah asked.

"A friend dropped me at the end of the road. He said he would give me an hour then be back to give me a ride back to town. See you around. Maybe I could call if I can't come out?"

Sarah nodded reluctantly. She loved her nephew, but he sure had created a lot of problems all those years ago.

CHAPTER 16

SOMEONE WAS OUTSIDE SKYLAR'S BEDROOM, sliding a note under the door, then gave a couple of brisk knocks until he heard her stir. Turning, the unseen man left, not waiting for her to answer.

Skylar had been laying there, thinking it was time to go slay her dragon. She had to tell Rhys she was starting to have feelings for him, depending on his reaction to the child they created. Or should she tell him about the baby? Would that influence his reaction when she told him she loved him?

"Just a minute," Skylar yawned, while getting up. Opening the door, she discovered no one there. Shaking her head, she went to step back when she saw the paper on the floor. Opening the paper, she saw what she had been waiting for. "Oh yes!" she exclaimed, excitement flooding her and giving her strength. It appeared that Lady was ready to foal.

Rhys should have come in to wake her. Running down the back stairs, not wanting to miss this experience, Skylar practically knocked the housekeeper over in her haste. "Oh Sarah, I'm so sorry. I was in a hurry."

In her motherly way, Sarah softly scolded her. "Now, don't you worry none about me. If I lived through those four boys' carrying ons, then putting up with you is a piece of cake. I bet you're ready for a bite to eat since you done slept through dinner. It's going onto ten o'clock girl! We need to get a little weight on them bones of yours. Now, what will you have, Miss Bree?"

"Oh no, I don't think I could eat."

"Nonsense, you set yourself right down here and I'll fix you something right quick," Sarah said. As she started to bustle around the kitchen, she couldn't help thinking that Miss Bree seemed so different, almost a different person. But Sarah supposed she had been through a lot. People changed, over time.

Skylar had to get going. "You don't understand, I can't stop. Lady's ready to foal. I just got a note. So I have to get to the stables now. I might miss it if I don't hurry."

Seeing the motherly look on Sarah's face, she tried edging closer to the door. Skylar didn't like to disappoint Sarah. "Look, I promise to have something when I come back up. For now, I'll grab an apple to eat on the way down, I promise."

"Get going with you, then. You're another little scamp, just like the rest," Sarah laughed.

Skylar bolted out the door, eating an apple Sarah had tossed to her on the way.

Sarah shook her head; she should be used to them by now. Looking out the window, she saw she was indeed eating the apple. Who was she to stop this girl? With all the gloom over these last few years, it was good to see the excitement. Miss Bree was so different now, who would have thought? She wouldn't have been caught dead going down to watch a birth before. There were times she didn't resemble the Bree she had known. Looks maybe, but nothing else was the same.

Skylar was breathless after running the whole way. Throwing the apple core off to the side, she went into the stables. Why wasn't anyone else here? Had Rhys been waiting by the front door? She knew he would check to see if she was still sleeping, and then come down himself.

Suddenly, in the pit of her stomach, it hit her. The danger she had felt was hanging over their heads was suddenly present, here right now. Skylar listened and heard nothing out of the ordinary. Glancing around carefully to see if all was in place, she couldn't help feeling as if she was being watched. Damn, why didn't she find one of the guys before coming down?

Being in such a hurry might be her downfall one day. While waiting for Rhys to find her, she talked to Lady to soothe her own nerves. "Well girl, will it be very long, do you think?"

"Not very long at all," John, Sarah's nephew said. "Glad you could make it. Dear Bree!" He laughed maniacally.

Startled, Skylar whirled around to face who was there. "Who are you? You scared me to death. Why didn't you show yourself before?"

"Ah, you don't remember me. I am crushed. You can't fool me though, you have to remember the name John. Aunt Sarah had to tell you about me," he said, his lip trembling in a fake pout.

Skylar was annoyed with him, and a little scared. Where was Rhys? About to turn her back on John, she looked into his eyes. They spoke volumes, mostly anger.

With a sneer, John stated, "Oh, scared are you? Well I'm doing more than that before we're through. As for showing myself, I had to make certain you were alone." He took a step closer to her, peering at her through the half-darkness in the stall. "Why couldn't you stay away? Just like before. You love him again. Damn you." He struck out at the side of the stall with is boot. "Answer me! You're in love with him again, aren't you? Dammit!"

"John," Skylar said, while trying to remember if she had met this guy. He was obviously crazy, and she needed to find a way to get him to understand the situation.

"Shut up, you good for nothing bitch. I got rid of you before. Well, I'll just have to do it again. One thing for sure, I will make damn good and sure you can't claw your way out this time. No sir, never coming back to bother me."

Skylar was berating herself for being a fool. She knew she shouldn't have come down by herself. What had Bree done to this guy?

She was trapped in a corner. He must have moved Lady to this far stall on purpose. It should have been a red flag. Trying to keep a clear head, remember what it was like growing up with a crazy mother, she reminded herself to never show fear. He would just feed into it.

If she could keep him talking, someone should come to make the rounds and discover them. At least she hoped someone would come.

When would Rhys go back upstairs, if he did tonight? If he didn't find her, would he know where to look? She was praying as she never had before. Sarah knew she was down here. Maybe, just maybe, she would tell Rhys. It was a long shot. Would Sarah go and ask if anyone else would be going down to the stables?

Skylar reminded herself once again – don't show fear. He would feed on it, and it would grow. "John, I don't understand this. Why are you angry with me? I think we could be friends, if Sarah is your Aunt." She kept her voice soft. "Why don't you want me here? If I knew you before, I'm sorry I don't remember. But after my accident, I'm not the same person you might remember."

Skylar was trying to edge past him while talking. She had been keeping her voice at a steady level the whole time so as not to arouse him. If she stayed calm, he might calm as well.

"Listen, let's spend some time talking, getting to know each other. Do you want to go up and see Sarah? We could get a cup of tea or something. Maybe we could become friends. You need to know, I'm learning what I was like before, and I don't want to be that kind of person now. I'm trying to merge the two of me to come out with a whole new person. Can you understand?"

Skylar had to try and keep this John talking. "John, please, talk to me. What went on before is something I have no way of knowing. I have no memory of that time in my life. I wish you could explain it and then we could talk to try and find some common ground. Whatever I did that made you angry, I'm very sorry about it."

John stopped and was trying to focus on her. What was she going on about?

John stepped into her path yet again. "If you could only have loved me this time, this wouldn't be necessary, you know. But no, you couldn't do it. Just like before. You chose him. You bitch, you loved him back then, and you love him now. You're nothing but a bitch, bitch, bitch."

"No John, part of me could love you because you are family to Sarah. Your aunt is a great person, but I don't really know you," Skylar said softly.

"Just shut your lying mouth." John was showing anger in his voice again.

Seeing Skylar was going to speak, John raised his hand as though to strike her. "Don't even begin your lies on me this time. I see the look in your eyes when he's around. It's there EVERY TIME, do you hear me, *every time*! Again and again I watch you moon around about him. Exactly what you did before. Wasn't … it … bitch? You lied back then, so you could tell Rhys all about me. But you never got the chance, did you? Surprise, surprise, it's not happening again."

Reaching out, he grabbed her arm. As Skylar struggled, he shoved her to the ground. He started to slap her and pull at her clothes. "Bitch … Bitch … Bitch," he repeated.

"John, you don't want to do this, please." Skylar was getting more frightened by the second as she struggled to protect herself from his hits.

"Don't bet on it, sweetheart. I'll finally have you before I'm through." John spoke with evil in his voice.

Skylar couldn't breathe. This couldn't be happening. It had to be a horrible nightmare. Shutting her eyes, she couldn't help thinking, where was everyone?

John wasn't on top of her any longer. Opening her eyes, she saw Craig was there and he was shouting something to her. Her ears were ringing, his voice sounded in slow motion. "Get … up … and get … the … hell … out of … here. Now move, dammit!"

Skylar had trouble pulling herself together, trying to get up and go. It took forever to process everything. Looking up as she heard footsteps, the words died on her lips. There she stood, looking at the menacing face of John. Her heart began to sink, or maybe it stopped.

Moving her head slightly, she saw red on his hands. Was that a shovel he was holding? Her mind was screaming in protest. He couldn't have hurt Craig!

John was laughing while he sneered. "Sorry sweetheart, he was going to interfere in our business. Should have stayed out of it." John chuckled. "Know something funny? This happened last time, too. Damn busy-bodied, nosey people. Ben went down the same way."

Shaking his head, John continued. "Well dear, it's time to go, almost eleven. Don't look sad, we'll continue our playtime later. Yes, somewhere else. That's it." He sneered in her face. "My, looking pale, aren't we? Fresh air is what you need. It will fix you right up, don't you think?"

He began pulling her from the stall. "Time is getting away from us, behind schedule. No more dawdling, we need to go. There will be no screaming, I'm warning you. I'll kill you right here. Do I make myself clear?"

Skylar was thinking he was totally mad. What pushed him to this? He said it was close to eleven; she had left the house after ten. It had been less than an hour, but it felt like forever had passed.

John let his fist connect with a splintering blow to Skylar's jaw.

As the black void was coming, she thought, *Is this the end?*

CHAPTER 17

IN THE LIBRARY, RHYS WAS laughing again. "Have you had enough, big brother?"

Laughter rang out from Alan as well. "Alright, I give up. But only cause it's close to eleven-thirty."

Rhys hadn't realized so much time had passed since checking on Skylar. He had wanted to talk with her tonight. She must have been totally wiped, sleeping this long.

Abruptly, Rhys asked the question pressing on his mind to Alan. "Alan, do you think she might be pregnant?"

Alan smiled, then, grinning at the worried expression on Rhys's face, Alan felt the mood need to be lightened. "By the way, when do you think this could have happened? Both of you have been hissing and clawing at each other for a couple of weeks. Didn't realize you got close enough to each other for it to happen."

"Dammit Alan, we haven't fought the whole time."

"Evidently not! I imagine you think you're the father."

"You're damn right I am! Will you quit with the laughing at me? This is serious. She was a virgin when she got here," Rhys said.

"Guess it means you might be the father after all. Will wonders never stop?"

Rhys shook his head, chuckling. "I guess you're right, but quit pulling my chain. I was being cocky, wasn't I?"

"Yes, you were."

"Hey, I'm going to be a daddy. She has to be about two or three weeks. I knew it. Hot damn, she is carrying my child." His eyes glittered as a smile lit his face.

"Rhys, don't start passing out cigars yet. And quit strutting around like a peacock," Alan laughed.

"Don't wait breakfast on us, we have a lot of things to talk over," Rhys said. "And a lot of making up to do. I mean, I have some ass kissing to do, and groveling."

Alan laughed once more. It felt good to see Rhys like this.

★★★

Jordan stopped Rhys by the stairs. "Why is John back here? I thought he was at the state hospital under evaluation."

Rhys was caught off guard, and reacted with suspicion in his voice. "What do you mean he's here? After hurting the horses the way he did, Grandfather banned him from being on the ranch."

"I saw him a little while ago talking to Sarah in the kitchen. It was around nine o'clock."

Rhys ran up to his room, instantly knowing Skylar wasn't there. Opening the door and seeing the ruffled sheets, with no Skylar, confirmed his fears. Panic was setting in. Could it have been John all this time? Why? He ran back down to the kitchen, not finding Sarah, so went to her room. He would knock until she answered. "Sarah! Open up!" He pounded his fists relentlessly on the door.

"Mr. Rhys, what's wrong?" Sarah was belting her robe as she opened her door to him.

"Was Bree down earlier?" Rhys asked.

"Yes, she was on her way for Lady's foaling time. She said she was meeting you at the stable." Sarah looked confused.

Rhys heard the back door crash against the counter with a deafening bang. He raced to the kitchen, just as the rest of the family was getting there. Craig was in the doorway, trying to stagger in. Blood was running down the side of his face.

Rhys reached out and made to grab him before he collapsed. Alan had Rhys lower him to the floor so he could look Craig over. Cleaning the wound, which he knew was hurting his cousin, Alan carefully examined his head.

Craig flinched, and opened his eyes.

"What the hell happened to you?" Rhys couldn't help demanding answers.

Craig could barely speak. "He's got her." Dropping back in pain, he gasped.

Rhys shouted, "Who has her? Dammit Craig! Don't pass out till we get answers. It's up to you to point us in the right direction."

Craig whispered one word. "John." He was unconscious then.

Sarah gasped, not wanting to believe it. "No, he said he was better. I know he wouldn't hurt Miss Bree. He said he still loved her, for helping him. And he's working for Mr. Anderson at the feed store."

Rhys was floored. John had done this. Why hadn't they thought of him this whole time? They must have forgotten he was here when Bree went missing. Now he had Skylar – Innocent, pregnant, kind Skylar...

His blood was boiling. "Sarah think, what time did Skylar come to the kitchen?"

Sarah looked mystified. "I don't understand, who are you talking about?"

"Damn! I mean Bree. What time was it?"

Sarah had to sit down. "Oh my word, she's not Miss Bree."

"Dammit, think woman! Her life may depend on us knowing everything we can. Ethan, call the cops while Sarah talks to us."

"I can't be positive, but it was close to, no. It was after nine. No, it was just going on ten, I know. John had been here talking to me and he said he had to get going, said he had things to do." Sarah paled, and choked on a sob, suddenly knowing what it was that John had to do.

They all knew what kind of danger Skylar could be in. They knew John since he had been young, and mean. Heading to the door, Rhys paused. "Alan, take care of Craig. Let him know what's happening. We are going to take care of things."

Rhys looked to Sarah. "I'm telling you, family or not, I'm going to find the bastard. If he hurt her, he may be paying with his life. He has a lot to pay for."

Sarah knew her nephew had been troubled throughout his life, and they tried to give him a loving home here on the ranch. At times he felt it was him, not the boys who should be here. He was here every day to help take care of things on the ranch.

The rest of the family headed to the stables to look for any clues to help. They found where John had fought with Craig. But there was another imprint of a smaller footprint, which inflamed Rhys. "If that's hers, then she is hurt. Damn him."

It had only been ten minutes since Craig came crashing into the house, but it felt as though hours had passed.

Ethan filled the ranch hands in on what was happening.

Returning outside, they found a few of the ranch hands there. "Hey boss."

"What is it?" He didn't have time for this.

"The Jeeps is missing," Jake said.

That information was vital, but knowing John had a vehicle also meant that he could be anywhere. "Thanks, Jake. Look around and try to determine which way he was headed." Rhys was trying to think of where the little weasel used to go to be alone.

"Sure thing Mr. Rhys."

She wouldn't be missing right now, if he had woken her earlier. Frustration was getting to him. "Damn, I can't tell which way. There's so many tracks in this drive, it could be any of them."

Paul walked over to him. "Calm down Rhys, we need to think and remember the places he used to go. We need to out think him, now. Following him won't help Skylar. We have to get ahead of him."

Tears were running down Rhys's face, he threw his head back in anguish. Turning to his family, he cried out, "I can't even think straight. Dammit! What am I going to do?"

They all felt Rhys's pain as their own. "Don't any of you remember something, anything? Anything at all?"

Ethan thought he might have a clue. "He was never gone that long when he would take off before. It has to be close."

"Think Ethan, can't you remember which direction?" Rhys needed a clue.

It dawned on Ethan. "I've got it, I think."

"Spill it, little brother, spill it."

"The old line shack up on the north pasture. He used it for a clubhouse when we were younger. Said it was a good place to think." Ethan paused as a ranch hand shouted.

"Boss? We have something!"

"Well, what is it, man?" Rhys wanted to get going.

"The Jeep has the donut on for a spare. It had a flat earlier. Makes the tracks look different. Looks like it's going over toward the backroad."

Rhys knew Ethan had been right.

"Boss, we're ready to ride with you."

Paul took action. "Rhys, we need horses. Wasn't Ben found out there when Bree disappeared? It will be an hour away using the backroads by Jeep. By horse you can get the in half the time." He turned to the men around him and shouted his order, "Men, saddle up some of the horses, fast!"

Rhys looked at his grandfather. "What's that got to do with the here and know?"

"Son, what if he had something to do with this back then?"

The ranch hands had the horses ready, and Rhys ran to them. Praying he was in time, and they were going to the right place, he leapt and swung his leg over the side of his favorite horse. When he looked around, he saw all the hands were going with him, and he said, "This is personal. I appreciate you wanting to help, but I need you to think of other places and check on them. Just in case we are wrong about this one."

Paul spoke then. "Some of you men go in each direction, where any of the line shacks are. I'm going to call around and see if they passed through anywhere close."

Rhys thought to himself, *God, please let me be in time. Don't let us miss him.*

"Be careful son, don't take unnecessary chances. I'll call your dad, also." Paul was heart-sick. How could this young man cause his family so much pain? After he had let him live here and have the run of the place for years? He understood that John was mentally ill, but why do this to the ranch he loved?

Ethan looked at his brother, who had his head bowed, knowing he was praying. "Rhys, we're ready to ride. The men all have walkies to keep in touch."

Rhys mounted up, looking to his brother. "Let's ride," he said, knowing they were on their way to meet the devil.

Paul and Matt went back to the house. All they could do was pray.

Matt stopped, and looked to the skyline. "Someone said that it's a good thing he never liked horses." He couldn't finish what was on his mind.

"Matt, it won't be as far on horseback for them, you know. I believe they will get to her on time. You must believe this, too."

CHAPTER 18

ON THE RIDGE, SKYLAR WAS struggling to get away. "John, please don't do this! You'll regret it later. I'm not who you think I am. Just listen! I AM NOT BREE!" It was as though he didn't hear her. Then, John gave her a fierce blow to the stomach, and Skylar doubled over in pain. Laying there, she felt it would be fruitless to try again right now. There was no reasoning with him.

Sneering, he said, "Get up again bitch, I'll kill you here and now. Would be a shame. Not ready, not ready, not ready. Have to dig again, you make me dig it again. You are a bad girl, why you make me do this again?" He laughed.

John looked right at her. "Daddy said everyone has to listen. I helped with the animals and the girls. I had to do things right or I was in trouble – you don't want daddy to get mad. Daddy had to show mommy how to be good. Mommy didn't listen though, all the screaming gave daddy a hurt head. Then he would have to punish her. I have to punish you now. Just like mommy, you don't listen very well." His laugh sounded like insanity.

Skylar knew he was completely over the edge; nothing was there but madness.

There was so much pain, and she was blacking out from time to time. So many things were running through her mind. First and foremost was the thought that Bree had probably come to love Rhys, in her own way. She hadn't left, because John had caused her to disappear. Just as he was doing to Skylar.

Would they think she was just like Bree, and just took off? Skylar wished Bree had lived. But then she and Rhys wouldn't be having a child. Blackness came again.

"Damn, bitch, you wake up. How will you enjoy this if you're sleeping? I want a piece of you first, so wakey wakey..." His pants were bursting with the wanting of Bree. All those other girls, never any good, none would be found.

Coming around, Skylar thought about her mother and Matt. What would their life have been like if they would all have been together? Or if Matt knew who she really was? Now it would be too late. Would Rhys show him the photo, tell him about her life? Would Matt believe Rhys?

Rhys wouldn't believe she left on her own. He knew better, didn't he? Was he looking for her, yet? Would her fate be the same as Bree's? The injustice of it; it wasn't fair.

In her heart, she was crying out. *Rhys where are you? Help me! Come and find me, get this madman. PLEASE HELP ME.* Blackness engulfed her again.

When she awoke, Skylar wondered how long it had been. John was still digging. *How deep was he going?* Did anyone know she was missing yet?

Was Craig dead or alive? Would he be able to tell the family what happened? Could she reason with John, should she try again? Would she have the strength or speed to get away from John?

"J– John?" her lips were swollen and speech practically was impossible. It was hard to see, so he must have beat her while she was unconscious. He had choked her as well, which made her throat hurt.

It started to rain, just what she needed. Skylar knew the weather was calling for a severe storm. Was God giving her cover so she would have a chance to escape? How could she when the numbness had begun setting in? In fact, she was so numb, there was not much pain now. It was funny. She was almost looking forward to death.

Would they all forget she existed?

★★★

The storm muffled the sound of the horses' hooves. The men had ridden hard to get to the line shacks. Rhys held up his hand when they were about a hundred yards from the shack he knew John would be at, thanks to Ethan's tip. There was a light ahead. "We better tie up the horses and go on foot from here. I don't want him to have any warning, no warning whatsoever," Rhys told the men.

What had John done to Skylar, or what was he doing? "I swear, he's going to pay for this. If he's killed her, the son-of-a-bitch is as good as dead himself," he murmured maliciously.

Creeping up on the shack, they heard digging, and the sound of someone muttering under their breath. They were around back. Rhys could see John's outline, digging against the dark sky, and a slumped form near his feet that must have been Skylar. Rhys motioned for the men to split up, to come at them from both sides. Upon reaching his corner, Rhys clearly saw Skylar. She was so still. Were they too late?

Upon seeing Skylar's prone figure, and not thinking, Rhys charged directly for John. Catching him at the waist, they both fell into the hole. Rhys thought it a fitting place for John to be ended here, and now.

Alan and Ethan reached Skylar's side to see if there was any life.

John was stunned. "What are you doing? You're going to ruin everything! We haven't even consummated our marriage. You're not wanted here! LEAVE US ALONE. She loves *me*."

Was Rhys hearing right? "You low down slime," he murmured. His voice alone could have been deadly.

Skylar's breathing was shallow. Alan knew she had to be moved out of the rain. Her skin was too cold; they needed to get her warmed up before she suffered from hypothermia. "Ethan, tell Rhys to knock him out already. And get him out of there before he *does* kill him. Tell him we have to move Skylar now."

Alan then turned to Jake. "Can you go to the shack and try to start a fire, and grab a couple of blankets?"

When both Ethan and Jake hurried off to carry out their tasks, Alan continued checking over Skylar's injuries. "Dammit Rhys, get over here now! I need help with her."

Ethan was coming back out when he saw lights coming up the road. "I assume the cops are almost here. Hasn't Rhys got out of that hole yet? I better get him out before he *does* kill the bastard, then the cops will arrest him on murder charges."

Quickly going over to the hole, Ethan said, "Rhys get the hell out now! Cops are here. Let the law handle him."

Rhys crawled out, feeling a great need to be with Skylar. "Don't feel sorry for him. I didn't kill him, not that I didn't want to."

Alan looked at the others. "We need to move now. Be careful carrying her."

Jake spoke up then. "The fire's going and I cleaned off the cot. Water is heating for whatever. Alan is she —"

"I don't know at this point, but it's bad. When the cops get here, have them radio for an ambulance, stat." He turned to Skylar once more.

Rhys struggled with all the questions whirling around his mind. Would there be any answers?

Ethan looked in. "The ambulances are under way. Should be hear in about five minutes." Returning outside, he finished talking with the cops. They had questions, which he had no answers for, but did his best to help them anyway.

Alan was trying to get Skylar to come around a little. "Come on sweetheart, fight for your life. We're here, we made it, don't let John win. Rhys is right here, we'll be going to the hospital soon." The ambulance arrived and the paramedics rushed into the shack. They recognized Dr. Cantrell, knowing he would have all the information they would need.

One of the paramedics gestured to Alan. "You ride along, since you already started treatment. We'll assist, then."

"Rhys let go of her hand, we need to load her up and get moving. You'll have to follow. There won't be room since I'm going to treat her during the ride," Alan told his brother.

One of the officers spoke. "Mr. Cantrell, we need to get your statement. We know you want to get to the hospital so we'll be quick. But we will be talking to you again later." Rhys highlighted the events of what took place. Then hightailed it to the hospital.

A few minutes later, as the police and paramedics were getting John out of the hole, they saw a skeleton. John was transported to the hospital with guards.

★★★

The local police soon discovered not just one skeleton, but many. They called in the FBI to help with the excavation. As they dug, it became apparent that the bodies had been wrapped tightly in plastic. How many would they find, and how many of them would be on the missing persons list. It was a graveyard. How long had John been doing this?

The team had spent two days digging out bodies, being careful and respectful. The first skeleton, was a female, with the remains of a child with it. All remains were sent for testing and comparison. A total of twelve bodies were recovered.

The officers couldn't believe what they found at the site. This was a peaceful town, nothing like this ever had occurred here before.

Another team was sent to the house he lived in, to see what was there. John had talked and laughed about a secret room and the extra special place in the floor that was his father's – now was his. It was unbelievable. He had a trophy room, filled with items that had to belong to the victims, jewelry, hair barrettes, and some woven hair. Were they all his or some of his father's was the question? A box of photos were found in a corner. Would any of the phots be of the victims from the ranch grave? The house had belonged to his parents. The things in the house were beyond what the mind could think of as evil. How much evil had this house seen. The FBI had a lot of investigating to do – and what all would come out was anyone's guess.

John had been treated at the hospital, then taken into custody for assault, attempted murder, and kidnapping. Charges were pending for all the other bodies. But it was more than likely that murder would soon be added to the list. But John wouldn't be standing trial; the doctors had declared him insane. The judge ruled he would be committed, no sense in wasting tax-payers' money on a trail. If, at a later date, if he was ever fit, then charges would be re-filed against him.

The FBI talked with Craig about the attack. The most asked question was why John felt the need to kill so many. They also asked if any of them noticed anything out of the ordinary about John. When the two teams were finally able to put everything together, they felt floored to the core by it all.

Craig reminded them about Bree, just in case one of the bodies was hers. But he knew it probably was. They had all thought this, but never voiced it out loud to Rhys. Ethan even shared that Skylar had been trying to help uncover what had taken place five years ago. The agents said they thought the first remains were those of Mrs. Cantrell and her child, but would know for sure after testing.

CHAPTER 19

AFTER RACING THROUGH THE EMERGENCY room doors, Rhys began searching for Skylar. Suddenly, he found a hand clamped on his arm.

"Dammit Rhys, you can't go room to room looking for her," Alan said. "I was in helping when one of the nurses came and told me my brother was likely to tear the place apart if someone didn't stop him. Let us do our jobs. You are getting in the way, which, in turn, will cause delays. Besides, you've checked every room but the one she's in. Rhys, she's in good hands. Tom is one of the best, as far as I'm concerned. I'm going back in now, so you can sit out here, chill out, and behave."

Rhys sighed. "I'll try to be patient, but can't promise."

"Fine. They need information at the desk. Do you think you could give most of what they need?" Alan said as he turned to go back in to help.

"I don't want to be far away, just in case she — "Rhys was afraid to finish his thought.

"Rhys, you have to do this, before you cause more problems. I'll send someone out as soon as possible. I have to get back in there."

Rhys nodded, then went to the front desk, giving them what he could. He returned to the waiting area, feeling like a caged animal. He should be with her, not standing in the hallway doing nothing. They had to save her, just had to.

Would they let him know? Dropping to his knees, he prayed as he had never prayed before – talking with God, pouring out his heart.

What is taking so long? He wondered. Turning, Rhys saw Paul and Matt get off the elevator.

With fear in his voice, Matt asked, "How's my daughter?"

Receiving no reply, he spoke again. "Rhys, say something."

"Alan's in helping, and it seems like it's been forever. He said someone will be out when they can." Rhys didn't feel up to talking.

"What was he doing out here talking to you? He should never have left her."

Rhys had no intention of telling why Alan had come out. "He'll be back out soon, then we'll know how Skylar is."

Stunned, Matt grabbed Rhys's arm. "Who the hell cares about someone named Skylar, or whatever? Dammit, I asked how my girl is. I want to know now. Where is she, and exactly how is she?"

Taking hold of Matt's hand, Rhys flung it off. Standing there, glaring daggers, it hit him what he said. "Matt listen, it is your daughter in there. But not the one you think. It's not Bree, but Skylar."

Ethan had been standing off to the side. "Well, I'll be dammed. She's his daughter?"

"I don't believe she isn't Bree. What are you trying to pull? Don't you tell me I don't know my own child!" Matt's fury was in his voice.

"That's just it, she is your child, but you didn't have anything to do with raising her," Rhys told him.

"But – "Matt stammered.

Rhys proceeded to tell him the story, not sparing Matt as he went on. Why should he, when he never liked the man to begin with?

"So what is her full name, and her mother's? If you know it and this is all true." Matt said while still doubting the farfetched story. It had to be Bree playing at one of her games.

"Her name's Skylar Evans and she said her mother's name was Larraine Stevens. Everyone called her Lainey though."

Sinking into the nearest chair, Matt seemed to go pale. She wasn't Bree, but how? Bree never knew Lainey's real name. So this was his child; he hadn't known. "I'll be, she was pregnant and didn't tell me. After all this time, to find out now. I wouldn't have left her if I had known. Rhys, where is she? We have to call her, let her know what's happening with Skylar. But how can we? You did say she was dead, didn't you?"

Taking a deep breath, Matt continued. "I guess it's all a shock of discovering I have another child. Lainey and I have a child together, I can't think clearly at the moment."

Alan was approaching them and Rhys jumped up to meet his brother. "How is she?"

"She isn't good, I won't lie to you. It's touch and go for now."

Rhys spoke, showing his emotions. "Damn, I should have killed the son-of-a-bitch. I can only hope he rots in prison, for this and everything else they are finding out about him."

"Rhys, I suggest you get ahold of yourself. Get rid of the hate, she will feel it, and it's not needed now. I want things as calm as possible for her. Do you understand?"

Alan was waiting for Rhys to agree. After receiving a nod, Alan proceeded. "They're moving her upstairs."

Turning, they found Paul Sr. holding Matt's arm. "I knew Rhys wanted to talk first, as is his right. So I sort of detained him."

Matt was angry. "I have a right to know what's going on! I'm her father, and he's nothing to her."

"You bastard," Rhys said under his breath.

"Both of you stop, now. It's a hospital, not an open field where you two can act like children instead of adults. If you both can behave, I'll finish talking about her injuries. And Matt, Rhys hasn't heard this, so quit staring daggers at me."

Rhys looked expectantly at his older brother, while Matt momentarily hung his head in shame.

"John did a number on her. He used her face as a punching bag. There are some broken ribs as well. Lots of bruising, over the next few days it will look worse. The bruising on the inside has us concerned, but the exposure had her core temp pretty low. She is still unconscious."

They were shocked, even though they had been with her before treatment. "Alan, what can we do for her?" Paul Sr. asked. He was the most level-headed and reasonable of the bunch right now.

"Sit and talk with her. Let her know she's safe and loved most of all."

Alan stopped. "Matt, I think Rhys is the person who will get through to her. The last thing she called out was for Rhys to help her. So, we will let Rhys help her. I hope you understand, you can still sit with her, but we both know she doesn't know you like she knows Rhys."

At Matt's nod of acceptance, Rhys started to head down the hall when Alan called out. "Rhys, you're heading in the wrong direction. I'll walk with you. We need to talk further, anyway." Alan led his brother off toward the elevator.

Alan saw Rhys's face pale at his words. "I didn't think you wanted the rest of the family to know. You know you were right about her being pregnant, but its touch and go for the baby also. I'm warning you so you can prepare, a decision might have to be made as to who is more important. To save Skylar, the baby might have to die. Will you be able to make the choice of losing another child? Think about it, and pray."

"I don't know if I can make a choice." Rhys had tears in his eyes.

"I'm just trying to get you prepared if a choice has to be made." Alan was holding Rhys's arm to keep him grounded.

Rhys had tears running down his face. "Why would he do this Alan, I can't grasp it?"

Alan was at a loss. "I'm not sure, my brother. Pray like you have never prayed before." Alan left Rhys there, knowing he had given his younger brother plenty to think about.

When Rhys reached the fourteenth floor, he checked room numbers as he went down the hall. Upon approaching Skylar's room, a nurse came out.

She laid her hand on his arm. "Sir, may I ask if you're related to the patient?"

"Rhys Cantrell, I'm her fiancée."

"Fine. Now you say it, you do look a lot like Dr. Cantrell." The nurse knew what this man was about to see.

"Yeah, brothers. I'm the better looking, he got the brains. Can I go in now?" Rhys had given the standard answer that come out automatically. It was snarky and didn't match the situation, but it couldn't have been helped.

"Yes, but don't be alarmed with what you see. There are lots of machines and she isn't in the best shape. I assume you talked with your brother?"

Rhys nodded. "I understand."

He said this, but it was still a shock. Rhys had thought Alan exaggerated, but knew in his heart his brother had tried to spare him some of her condition. To think he might not have seen her alive again. If he had anything to do about it, she was here, in his life, to stay.

Rhys's throat was raw from talking all through the night to her. She needed to know what was in his heart. He had to remind her that they weren't finished by a long shot. Finally, feeling as if he couldn't wait for her to come back to him any longer, he called her a coward, and she was one if she couldn't fight just one more time and come back. *Don't let John win this war*, he thought.

When it didn't work, Rhys broke down and cried. As his tears fell, they landed on Skylar. But then, just slightly, he felt her finger twitch beneath his. Was she hearing him, understanding? Rhys hoped so, for all the world he hoped so. Rhys buzzed for the nurses.

Chapter 20

The remains of Bree and the child were released to the family after a long investigation. It still wasn't over, but they had all the evidence and data they needed to lock John up. Rhys couldn't be bothered with a service now, though. He asked for his ex-wife and child to be buried in the family plot and for the church to put up a marker. Later, maybe they could have a memorial service for them.

His main concern was for Skylar. Rhys and Matt kept a vigil by her bed, and prayed for God to spare her. Both had just found this person, and neither wanted to lose her yet.

Skylar was in and out of consciousness for the first few days. Around noon of the third day, she came out of it, but was weak. Rhys's face greeted her, which made her feel safe. Was she dreaming? Rhys wasn't speaking, why? She tried to speak, but nothing came out. Trying to swallow, she turned her head and saw Matt sitting there. Did Matt know about her?

She guessed she lived through John's attempt at killing her. Skylar had tears running down her face, but everyone else in the room did, too. Rhys took her hand, rubbing it. "I thought I lost you, I —"

Matt looked at this girl, her and Bree could have been twins, just as Rhys said. Seeing the color of her eyes, Lainey's sky-blue eyes he fell in love with, his heart almost burst with emotion. Would he get a chance to spend time with her? "Rhys?" He asked when he heard the stutter in the young man's voice.

Rhys seemed to know Matt wanted, no needed, to speak with Skylar. It probably would be better to let them have this time. He should be helping with the services for Bree and the baby. Many thought it was cruel that he couldn't seem to spend a moment on them, when just a few short weeks ago, he was willing to sacrifice a woman's safety to find them. Nodding at Matt, he said, "I guess I'll go out to the ranch for now. I have a few things needing done. Sweetheart, he needs to talk to you." Kissing her forehead, he turned to go.

"Rhys?" Skylar didn't know what to say.

"I'll talk to you later. I love you."

Matt looked from one to the other, feeling a little bad at separating them, but also glad Rhys was giving them this time. "Well, daughter ... I hope you don't mind me saying that? Rhys told me what he knew. Finding out you are Lainey's child – and mine – It blows my mind." He paused, choked with emotion. "It's amazing"

Skylar saw love in his eyes when he spoke her mother's name. So what kept them apart? He couldn't know what kind of person she turned out to be, the radical change she went through. "Matt, tell me about your relationship with my mother. I need to know what happened, what caused her to be like she was. An explanation about why you weren't part of my life."

He sat for a few minutes, remembering. Rhys had said Lainey wasn't good with Skylar. Why had she changed so much? Regret for all he missed over the years flooded him with guilt because he hadn't kept after Lainey. Why had he believed the last phone call?

"So you want the story, do you? You deserve some explanation, no doubt. I doubt I have all the answers you want though. Rhys told me how she treated you, it was unbelievable he was talking about the same woman I knew before we split. Why we weren't together, though? I can't tell you the reason. Believe me, I never knew about you. If I would have, nothing, I mean nothing, would have kept me out of your life." As Matt slipped into his memory, his eyes took on a soft sheen.

"Lainey and I met at a business dinner. She was a secretary for one of the other companies present. We were attracted to one another from the moment we looked at each other. Love at first sight. Never did I think, even for a moment, it would happen to me. But it did happen for both of us, or so I believed.

"I saw your mother every chance I had while I was in town. Our time only lasted six or seven weeks, depending on how you look at it. Not to make light of it, we only slept together once. It happened the night I was going to ask her to marry me. I had it all planned, nice meal, and then I would pop the big question.

It all got turned around, though. We didn't leave her place, and you were created. I was called home, as a widower with a three-year-old daughter, there was no question of going. I had told your mother, Bree was spoiled rotten. Which I admit was my own fault, being out of town on business a lot, I let her do what she wanted so I wouldn't feel as guilty. The hired help gave in to her so they didn't make me angry. I tried to give her everything, to make up for losing her mother, and then me to business.

"Anyway, the phone call indicated Bree was gravely ill. At first, I figured she was pulling another stunt to get me home. But the housekeeper assured me, she was taken to the hospital. Your mother said for me to go and take care of my daughter. I got home as quick as I could, and found she had a form of meningitis.

"On one of our phone calls, your mother said to ask Bree how she would feel about having another woman in her father's life. When Bree started getting better, I brought up the idea to her. I told her about Lainey and shared how I felt about her. Bree was overwhelmed by the idea of having a new mother, and couldn't wait to meet her. She had me call Lainey to have her come out and stay with us right then."

Matt paused to look at Skylar. He hadn't been paying attention to her. How was this affecting her? Seeing she wasn't torn apart, he went on. This daughter seemed to be made of stern stock.

"I called and talked with Lainey every other day during Bree's convalescing. I sensed a growing distance in her voice, and she didn't want to talk about our plans. In one of our conversations, I asked if everything was alright. She assured me, she was fine, just a lot on her mind.

"The distance made everything worse, and when I asked her if she could be carrying our child, she denied it. She said if she was carrying a child, wouldn't she have let me know? I had said yes, I knew she would have. And to think, I believed her."

Matt shook his head, still trying to wrap his head around Lainey's lies and the fact that Lainey had indeed been pregnant with his child.

"Our calls became stiff and quiet, and I was stumped as to why. Finally, she asked me not to call anymore. She had found someone else, and they were getting married. It was like getting sucker punched. I thought it had been love and that we were going to be a family.

"But what could I do but honor Lainey's request? I threw myself into work and my daughter became distant and cold. I tried to put Lainey out of my mind, but never managed to forget her. Part of me still loves her and always will."

Suddenly, Matt shifted in his chair and back to the present. He looked somberly at Skylar. "Do you think we might be able to go on from here? You don't have to answer now. Finding each other was a shock to both of us. Not an unpleasant one, but a happy one as far as I'm concerned. To think, I have a new daughter, and even though you're twenty-five, I want to buy cigars and give them out. I know it sounds silly, but I couldn't be happier right at this moment. I hope you will become happy about having me for a father."

Skylar hadn't said a word, letting Matt tell his story. She didn't know what she was feeling. This didn't answer many questions. "It's a lot to take in," she said simply. She was unsure how to respond.

"Well, what do you think, can we be friends? We got to know each other some out at the ranch, so it's not like we just met. I think it will be enough for present, don't you?" Matt asked with hope.

"I'm not sure what to say right now," Skylar said with hesitation.

"I think we've talked enough for today. Give us this chance, please. There's much to deal with, isn't there?" Matt tried again.

Skylar found herself wanting to be enfolded in her father's arms. She started to cry, and then Matt broke down as well. And then he was hugging her and rocking her like a child. "We will get through it, we'll do it together," Matt said with choked emotion.

Skylar pulled back. "It just doesn't make sense to me about my mother. If she loved you enough, why hide her pregnancy?"

Alerted to Skylar's heightened emotion due to the quickened beating of the heart rate monitor, a nurse came in to check on Skylar. "I think she has had more than enough for one day. I tried to let you have more time, but she looks done in. We don't want her to overexert herself."

Matt knew the nurse was right, and leaning down, he kissed his daughter's cheek. "I will see you later sweetheart. Get some sleep, and know you are loved."

Skylar murmured, "I'll remember," and was asleep before Matt left the room. It seemed right, now, to be able to accept him as her father. It gave her a sense of peace, knowing he hadn't left without another thought for her. She hoped he understood everything she was feeling.

Chapter 21

It was decided the services for Bree and the baby were to be held on July 23rd.

When Skylar found out, she made the decision to sign herself out of the hospital if she wasn't ready to be discharged. Matt and Alan couldn't believe she wanted to do this. They had to make her see sense, after going through so much.

"Skylar, you can't be serious. Do you think you're fit enough to leave the hospital yet?" Her father asked.

"I know how you feel, but I know what I want. I have to be there for Rhys. He will need me with him now, more than ever. He shouldn't have to be alone at this time. Don't ask me not to do this, it won't do any good." Skylar told Matt.

Knowing he was getting nowhere, he turned to the other man. "Alan, can you talk some sense into this stubborn girl?" Matt's voice had raised as he finished.

Skylar faced them both. The look she gave them would've quieted most people. Alan looked at her and laughed. "You know something, you're giving us the same look Rhys uses when he won't listen to reason. The both of you have it down to a science."

"You both listen," Skylar said stubbornly. "If nothing else, she was my sister. I didn't get to meet her, but I did get to know a lot about her these last couple of months. In fact, I lived her life. I pretended to be her, and I feel attached to her. I love Rhys with my whole heart, and we will get through this together. He needs us all there with him, united as a family."

"Sweetheart, we understand how you feel," Alan said, smiling.

Skylar wasn't going to let him finish. "Alan, you're a doctor. Why can't I be released into your hands?"

"I don't know, Skylar. Chelsea wouldn't like me having you in my hands. She likes my hands only on her."

"Damn you, Alan, be serious!" Skylar was all determination and fire. "Couldn't you watch over me? If I start to feel unwell, then I promise I'll tell you right away, I promise."

"I guess it could work. Let's talk with your doctor first." Alan stated.

Matt began to smile. "You know something Alan, I was never able to say no to Bree, so heaven only knows why I even imagined I could say no to this one."

Alan laughed. "I guess I had better go and make arrangements to have you sprung then. Now, don't you guys go anywhere until I get back."

Skylar threw a pillow at him. "You're just as crazy as the rest of your family." Her smile fell as she realized what she had said.

"Hey, try and forget him for now. John wasn't blood-related, and he is getting the help he needs. Don't feel sorry, you didn't say anything wrong. Now, behave until I get back."

"Okay, I will. I don't think I could escape without the two of you."

★★★

They left the hospital a few hours later and headed to the ranch. Matt took Skylar's arm to help her into the house. She was a bit wobbly, but Alan gave a nod, and raised his eyebrow at her. They paused in the foyer to rest for a moment.

Alan heard voices coming from the library, and turning to Skylar, he spoke. "I suppose you hear them, too. I know I shouldn't ask, but, do you prefer to go up to the bedroom or into the library?"

"I think I'd like to go and surprise Rhys. Then he will know I'm home and here for him," Skylar answered with a smile.

"I knew what you were going to say, not sure why I wanted to hear it." Alan just shook his head.

Skylar looked at Alan. "Listen smart mouth, I'll go rest after I see him, and he knows I'm right here and going to be fine."

Alan laughed, then turning to go up the stairs, the three of them headed to the library. Skylar stopped them short of pushing the door open. Had she heard what she thought?

Skylar held her hand up to silent the men. The three of them could hear what was being talked about. It was getting very emotional. Afraid of what she would hear, but more afraid of what she didn't know before, a part of her didn't want to believe what she was hearing.

"Grandfather, how could I have failed her? I just as much killed her and the child as John did. Did you know, they told me it was a boy? I had a son one minute, and he was gone the next! Why didn't I pick up on what John was like? I may as well dug the hole and put them in it!" Even through the door, the distress and emotion was evident in Rhys's voice.

"Rhys, son you didn't do any of this – none of us knew just how mental John was." Paul spoke with chocked emotions in his voice.

"Damn, why did I fail her? Dammit, why?" Rhys's grief flooded out of him.

Paul needed for Rhys to listen. "Son, it's over now – it will always be part of your life. But you don't need to let it define your life from here on out.

"Just think, he cheated us out of all the time of being a family. How much more can I let him take from me? I've lived in hell for the last five years." Rhys broke down.

Alan went to reach past Skylar; it was time to let Rhys know they were there. Skylar put her hand on his arm to stay his motions. Shaking her head no, she then pointed back toward the foyer. She wanted to lay down.

Reaching her room, she sank down. There was no fight in her. "Please don't let him know we heard that."

Skylar was close to tears, barely holding it together, but she quickly made decisions on how to handle things. Looking up at the two men, who had worried expressions on their faces, Skylar murmured, "I'm tired and need to rest, but want to talk with you both first.

"I'll be staying until the services are over, then I'm going away for awhile, unless Rhys shows me he wants me here. I need to pull my own life back into perspective. There are so many things, I have to deal with."

Alan grimaced. "You can't, Skylar. You need to be looked after."

"Matt will look after me, won't you, father?" Skylar asked with choked emotions.

"Is there any need for you to even ask, daughter?" Matt stated with a grin spreading across his face. He couldn't believe that she would trust him so much to let him take her from this place and help her through her grief and fear.

"I don't know Skylar, after what you heard downstairs, maybe —"Alan was very concerned with how pale she seemed.

"Alan, I'll be fine, I'm an adult, you know. You think I should wait, but let's see how I'm holding up after the services."

"Alright, if I feel you're not ready, you won't be going. Even if I have to lock you in your room. Understood?" Alan asked firmly.

"Yeah, I understand," Skylar answered.

Alan looked her over. "I realize you do need time, and I'll keep what happened earlier to myself, but only so long. I won't promise not to tell Rhys if he asks me straight out what's bothering you, though."

Skylar rose from the bed and crossed to the window. How many times had she stared out this window since coming here? "Alan, you must know, I would never ask you to lie to your brother. Not about anything."

She had a favor to ask, but should she ask it of him? Would he be willing to help her? There was only one way to find out. "Would you do something else for me?"

"Depends on what it is."

"If things turn out, and I do leave after the services…If I write a letter, do you think you could give it to Rhys?" She hurried on talking before he could answer. "But only give it to him when and if he asks about me."

Alan considered the options and ramifications of Skylar's request. "Yes, I can do it for you."

"Thanks! I realize he probably needs time himself. He has to grieve for Bree and his child before getting on with his life. My being around might make it awkward for him. He would try and keep me from being hurt, and it wouldn't help him. He needs to get past it, if he can, and I would only be a reminder of it all.

"It's crazy, but it's a fact, we both need to heal. Before we can be any good for the other." Skylar was close to tears.

Alan nodded understanding. "You're pretty smart for all the older you are."

"Thanks for the compliment, but right now I feel as though I'm ninety. And I probably look close to it also, with this face."

"You're still beautiful, even with the black eyes," Alan said with a grin.

Skylar began to cry.

"Listen, I didn't mean to make you cry. I want to tell you, if you do go, stay in touch with us. No matter what else happens, you have to promise me this." At her nod, Alan seemed satisfied, and he turned and left.

Matt smiled at Skylar. He couldn't get over the fact she wanted him to take care of her. He hadn't listened to what else was being said, he was so happy with what she said about him. "Honey, I can't tell you how glad I am you decided to come home with me. To be able to take care of you and have time to get to know one another better is just what we both need. It's more than I could have hoped for when I found out you were my daughter. Think, we can build a relationship we were both cheated out of."

Skylar shook her head as Matt was talking. "No, I'm not going with you per say. We will be leaving the ranch together, but I won't be going to your home."

She didn't give him a chance to speak. "Please, let me have my say. I can't handle more right now. I am stressed to the breaking point. Right now, this relationship you want, isn't going to happen. Don't take me wrong, maybe in a few weeks or a month. Give me some time."

Skylar saw the hurt on Matt's face. "Please, I don't mean it the way it sounds. I just have to pull myself together first. No one else can do this for me. It's something I have to do on my own. I've played at being Bree for the last how many weeks? And I'm scared of what I may have become. I need to know if there still a Skylar and start being me again.

I want to be your daughter, and I want you to be my father, but right now, I don't remember who I am."

Matt took a deep breath. "I think I'm beginning to understand. I wasn't there for you, and it's what hurts the most."

"You didn't know. I want to go back home for a couple of weeks. I can't promise anything at this point. All I'm asking you for is to give me time to sort out myself. Don't think of my leaving as an end, but a start at a new beginning for us all."

Matt nodded, knowing it was futile to argue with her. "I do understand more than you know. Don't think you can't tell me anything. I might not like what I hear, and make no mistake, I will tell you, but I'd rather it be said than have a wall put up between us. Be honest with yourself first and foremost, then worry about the rest of us. I'll do whatever I can to help you, whether you want me to or not."

Matt opened his arms, waiting to see if Skylar would take a step. A moment passed, but then she rushed into his embrace, needing to feel it more than she realized. Matt hugged her, not wanting to let go, or let anything hurt her again.

"Thanks Matt." Tears were coursing down her face.

"It's all worth it, if we can get past this. I'd probably agree to almost anything. You get some rest and I'll see you in the morning before the service. Sleep well."

Matt somehow managed to keep a tight rein on his emotions until he left the room and shut the door slowly, but firmly, behind him.

Skylar decided to wait until morning to compose her letter to Rhys. Things would be clearer after some sleep. Around midnight, something woke her, giving her a fright. Seeing it was Rhys, noticing he didn't seem right, she asked, "Are you alright, Rhys?"

He looked at her as if she was a stranger. "That's right, Alan said something or other about you signing yourself out of the hospital. I can't imagine why you did it. Just go back to sleep." Rhys turned away from her, trying to be strong, knowing he was close to the breaking point. If he tried talking he felt he would shatter. The lines kept blurring, Skylar and Bree – Bree and Skylar – they both could have been in that hole in the ground. He brought them both here to the ranch to be safe, and instead put them in the path of a madman. The guilt and grief were consuming him.

"You can't imagine why?" Skylar responded, unable to control her own emotions, even though she knew how much Rhys was hurting. "She was my sister, and I wanted to be here for you." How could he dismiss her so casually? It was impossible to lay in the same bed as him. She got up and went down to the library to sit out the rest of the night.

What they had shared...was it all make-believe for him? Or was his grief talking? It seemed strange at this moment. It felt like they were so close before, but now so far apart. When he came in, it felt like they could have been strangers passing in the night.

Even stranger, Rhys hadn't asked where she was going when she got up. For so long, he had to know every move she made. And he hadn't asked how she was feeling. Come to think about it, he hadn't even glanced her way at all. It was if he didn't want to look at her. The pain wasn't just from her injuries now. Was he so lost in his own grief that he couldn't really see her?

All of the time and things they shared, could it have been due to her resemblance to Bree? The more she thought, the more she felt it was possible. She had been used her whole life, why be surprised if she was being used now? Well, it was going to be a long night. Might as well write the damn letter and be done with it, it was the perfect time.

The next morning, Skylar kept to herself, not wanting to see anyone before the service. Especially Rhys, since he acted like she wasn't there. She knew in her heart he was hurting, but dammit, so was she.

The service was very brief. The pastor said a few words and everyone went back to the house. *Is that all the service was going to be?* Skylar thought.

Matt sought Skylar to talk to her. "Sorry we didn't get to talk this morning."

"Don't worry about it, you needed to say goodbye to Bree. I understand. It gave me time to pack and get my things ready."

"Are you sure you want to do this?"

"Why ask? You never cared for the family anyway. Why show concern now?"

137

"The concern isn't for them. I just want what's best for you. I know you love him, so why leave at all?"

With tears in her eyes, Skylar said, "How would you know what's best for me, do you know me? Just don't ask!"

Matt felt like she had slapped him in the face, but she was right. "I guess, whenever you're ready, we'll go."

"As soon as I've spoken to Alan, I'll be ready," Skylar said firmly.

"Fine, I'll see about having the car brought around front."

Skylar went on. "Please have my luggage brought down to the car, it's by the bedroom door."

At Matt's nod, Skylar went in search of Alan. Finding him in the rose garden, and alone, she approached. "I'm glad to find you alone."

"You're really going to do this, aren't you?" He asked.

"Alan please, I feel I have no choice in the matter." Skylar was close to tears.

Alan felt frustrated. "Can't you talk to him first?"

"No. If you had been there last night, then you would know why." Opening her purse, she pulled out a sealed envelope. Handing it to him, looking into his eyes, she whispered, "You will keep this in a safe place?" She suddenly let out a great sob.

Alan had to try again. "Skylar, I wish you would reconsider what you're doing."

With tears she said, "With a little luck, you might not have it very long. Seriously, you know it's time for me to leave, but I'm going to miss this family so very much."

"So why leave and cause this pain? Things have a way of working out."

"Alan, would you rather I stayed, and end up hurting even more?" She asked.

Sighing, Alan shook his head. "No, I don't."

"You know all of you guys have been a family to me, more than my own ever was." Skylar made a choked sound, and then continued. "Do you think it would be alright, if I'd ask you for a hug?"

"Need you even ask?" Alan said while opening his arms.

Skylar hugged him tightly, and then stepped away. "You'll give my love to the rest of them, won't you?"

"You bet." Alan felt like he was losing a sister.

Turning, Skylar started to walk away. Alan had something else to say. "Skylar, wait."

"Alan?" She said in confusion.

He had to know. "What about the baby? Did you put that in your letter to Rhys?"

"Alan, don't make this harder for me than it already is. But to answer your question, no." At his gasp, Skylar continued. "Let me explain. I knew you knew, since John and all. This isn't something I'm ready to tell him yet. Please, respect my decision, I'm begging you not to tell Rhys."

Alan gave a nod, he had no need to tell his brother something he already knew. Skylar paced the length of the path, trying to put her reason into words. "If I am meant to be with Rhys, I want it to be because we love each other beyond anything else. Not due to me being pregnant. If he knew, we would be married, and nothing else would matter. And I'd never be able to leave him. I love him too much. I won't know if we're together for us or for the child's sake. And I want him to love me. Truly love me. I don't want him to feel obligated.

"Trust me, if we both don't get our lives back on track, we won't be good for anyone. I'll do the right thing, and tell him about the baby later. Never would I keep his child from him. I know what it's like meeting your father for the first time when you're twenty-five. It is enough to drive you crazy.

With tears running down her face, she continued. "I do have to go. Do you think, if I have any trouble … ah … ah … do you think maybe, I could call on at least one of the Musketeers? If you don't hate me over this?"

Alan grabbed her in another hug. "You crazy fool, what do you think? You have to know we all love you. If you call, I'll be there for you as fast as I can." He held a sobbing Skylar for a moment more, before she pushed herself away, then fled.

Chapter 22

It had been a long day. They landed at Altoona airport around four p.m., and then proceeded to Lakewood. As evening approached, Matt stopped the car in front of the apartment Skylar had rented when coming to town. Matt helped her with her bags, all the while intending to talk sense into her about her plans.

He was imploring Skylar to change her mind. If she wasn't going with him, she needed to let him stay so he could take care of her. "You know I don't like that you are staying here on your own. Or going back to those Blackwells. Can't you reconsider going to my home?"

Skylar glared. "First off, those Blackwells are the people who have loved me from the start of our relationship. Don't you ever say their name in that tone again. My decision is final, either accept it, or don't. I'm doing this."

"Dammit, you just got out of the hospital a few days ago. I doubt you're as well as you think you are," Matt argued back.

"Quit it! This is getting you nowhere," Skylar voiced.

"Think about, I'm your father. Who better to take care of you? I was cheated out of all the years before now. I deserve to help you now." Matt was glaring at her.

Skylar was fuming now. "I absolutely refuse having you lay a guilt trip on me for something I had nothing to do with, just to get your own way. I didn't know about you before, so there is no way, and I stress *no way*, that I'll stay with you out of guilt."

"I didn't mean —" Matt was trying to back pedal.

Skylar wasn't letting him off the hook. "Oh yes, you did."

"Yeah, maybe I was trying anything I could to get you to do what I wanted. I do want to help, if you'll let me," Matt said with a heavy heart.

"If I stay here, and let you stay, how long before you treat me like the child you missed out on? Telling me what I can and can't do. Whether you're my father or not, it doesn't give you the right to try and bend me to your thinking and wishes. I'll tell once more, the guilt trip was a nice touch, but not enough for me to change my mind. So drop it."

"Skylar, sorry. I want you to stay, what more can I say." Matt was feeling defeated.

"I told you this whole trip I need time to sort myself out. Can't you give me this time?" She was ready to shout.

Matt knew he was not going to win this one.

"I promise we won't lose touch. I will call and talk with you. So get that defeated look off your face, and let's look to the future. Now give me a hug, then you better get going." Skylar had to be firm.

Matt hugged her, not wanting to let go. Skylar stepped back and went into her apartment.

Skylar's plan of leaving right away for the Blackwells was put off. She found herself sitting, waiting, but waiting for what? Maybe for Rhys to come and get her? If she didn't think it so serious, it would be funny.

After a couple of days, Skylar felt it was time for a visit. Calling Harry and Jean, she let them know she was on her way. Should she pack everything? Or would she be coming back to this town. What was here for her? Just her whole new life, Rhys, and the love she felt for him.

Had he missed her yet? That was a question she didn't know if she wanted the answer to.

If Rhys did get his head together, she told him in the letter she was going back to the beginning to find the real Skylar. Would he know what she meant? Should she call, no …

Deciding to head out on one last walk around town before heading back home, she found herself in front of the very place where this adventure had begun, Sam's Place. It had been nine weeks ago, but it felt like an eternity now. Going in, Skylar got a cup of coffee to go. It was time to go back to the apartment and start her drive to Maple Grove, half way across the state of Pennsylvania.

The Blackwells had been her rock from the time she was sixteen. They were the two people she could depend on, no matter what. Skylar thought she had better get started on the road, as she didn't want to stop over anywhere.

The trip seemed to be taking forever, but finally, she reached the outskirts of her hometown. Driving on, she found the one special driveway she had been watching for. This was like coming home to her haven.

The Blackwells recognized the car pulling into the drive. Opening the front door, they went to the car as Skylar parked. Jean was crying as she hugged the breath out of Skylar. "Skylar, Skylar, you've come home. I've been worried sick. We've missed you terribly."

"Let us look at you girl," Harry said, and then a look of horror crossed his face. "Who the hell? I'll kill the bastard. Just you tell me who did this, and I'll take care of them."

It dawned on Skylar what he meant; she had completely forgot about her face. With a choked voice, she spoke. "Please, not now. Can we talk about this later? I don't want to talk out here on the doorstep."

Jean nodded and began to lead Skylar into the house.

"Do you think, maybe, I could stay here for a few days?"

"Sweetheart, you never have to ask! We told you this is your home and we have always wanted you here. You're the daughter of our hearts, and we love you," Jean stated.

"Yeah, and you're the parents of my heart, and I love you both. I'm really tired right now. So, if you don't mind I really need to lay down and try and sort some stuff out."

"Skylar, I'm so sorry. Come on, let's get you upstairs so you can rest. Do you want a cup of tea or anything to take up with you?" Jean was worried about her girl. There was more than meets the eye going on.

"Thanks Jean." Skylar was close to tears.

"No more talk right now. Harry can you go grab her bags out of the car?" Jean asked.

Skylar needed to say something more. "I have so much I've got to talk with you about, I'm not sure where to begin."

Jean gave her another hug. "When you're ready, we'll be here to listen. Don't force things. You get some rest and then we'll see you later. We'll help you sort out things the best we can if you want help."

"Oh Jean," Skylar's lips trembled.

"Now, none of that for now. Get into bed and have a rest. I'll be downstairs when you're ready." Jean's heart was heavy.

"Okay. And Jean, I just want to say I love you guys again."

"And we love you, sweetie. See you in awhile." Jean left, quietly pulling the door closed.

After resting for a couple of hours, Skylar went downstairs in search of Jean and Harry. It was time to tell them of the last two months. With each piece of the news, Harry became angrier and angrier. Skylar had one heck of a job trying to keep him from going out to find each and every person responsible for all her heartaches. He wanted to give them all their just desserts. If they had been any kind of people, they wouldn't have let her get involved after finding out who she was. Especially after what they had done to start with.

Skylar talked to Jean about being pregnant. Together they told Harry, who wasn't happy a first, since the guy had taken advantage of their Skylar. Once he calmed down though, he realized they were going to have a grandbaby to spoil rotten.

Jean looked at Skylar. "I think we should call and make you an appointment to get you checked over."

"Could you call? I need to lay back down." Skylar answered, part of her was still numb. Would she find herself again, feel whole? It had been hard playing at being Bree; it was even harder trying to get back to being herself. It was ironic, the very thing Rhys had said was to come true. When this started, he said she had to become Bree in every sense. There would no longer be a Skylar Evans to speak about. It would be as if she never existed. How right he had been? She lost her own person in this whole episode.

★★★

Two weeks flew by, but Skylar was feeling restless. Something, or should she say someone, was missing. She wasn't finding what she needed here. Maybe she would drive down the coast till she felt like stopping. Jean and Harry were going to pitch a fit. How could she convince them she needed this?

Her life seemed like it could have been a movie on TV.

Why couldn't she understand how they felt? She had the shit beat out of her, and she was over two months pregnant. She didn't need to be gallivanting all over the country. "You just came home to us a couple weeks ago."

Skylar hugged Harry. "I told you when I came, it was just to pull myself together, and visit with you, my family."

"I should have known. You didn't bring much in the car with you. I ignored the fact. But it was in the back of my mind, that you weren't staying. You didn't think I noticed, did you? My heart aches for you. You have gone through so much and we couldn't help." Harry's voice wavered.

"Oh Harry, I never could pull one over on you. But you both have helped me more than you think. I just need something, I don't know what though."

Harry felt he was losing this argument. "I know you're not better, young lady. You pretend, try and play a good game. But you forget, I do know you better than anyone else. So, I don't want any back talk from you."

Skylar knew he was feeling emotional. "Harry, I am going. I need to do this."

"I won't have it. Dammit, do you hear me?" Harry said as the tears in his eyes began to run down his face.

"Not only do I hear you, I imagine the whole neighborhood did." Skylar felt light-hearted. Looking at this man, who had always been there for her, she grinned. "You know something, I may have been hurt, but I'm alive. And very thankful for it. I grew up a lot over the last couple of months. The world is full of ugly places and uglier people, but it's the only one we have. I do still want to find the good in people, though. You taught me that. You have to remember, without the two of you, I wouldn't have had a life worth speaking of."

"Listen, here young lady." Harry tried to continue.

"No, don't say anything. I haven't finished. I found so much through this. I could never be sorry about it, but I wouldn't want to go through it again. If I hadn't been in the wrong place at the wrong time, or looked so much like someone else, I wouldn't have found a love like the two of you have. Meeting Rhys was worth everything." Skylar rubbed her belly.

Jean understood Skylar's emotions better than Harry. Harry didn't want to listen. In his mind, Skylar wasn't going anywhere else. But in the end, Jean was on her side. So much so, she argued long and hard with her husband that Skylar needed some room.

Skylar looked at these people, who had her heart. "You know you will always be a part of my life, don't you?"

"Yeah, I guess we do," Harry admitted reluctantly.

"Harry, there is something else I haven't told you guys." Skylar saw Harry grow pale.

"No it's not bad, I found my biological father through the whole mess. You will always be the father of my heart, nothing has changed. And Jean, you are the mother of the same said heart." Skylar began to cry along with the older couple.

Jean and Harry knew their hearts would be joined by love to this girl forever.

Harry pulled himself together somewhat. "You have to promise me that you'll call at least every other day and let us know how you are and where you are. No more secret adventures which keep you out of contact with your family. Agreed?"

Sending a prayer to God for putting these two in her life, Skylar answered. "It is little enough to ask of me. I love you both so much it hurts. Whether I'm here or miles away, our hearts will always be joined by the love we share."

CHAPTER 23

THE FOLLOWING MORNING, SKYLAR DROVE off. Harry still wasn't sure about her going, but was resigned to it. He didn't like that she had no destination in mind.

Skylar's days turned into a pattern. Getting up, she would drive for a couple hours, stop to check out the area and getting a bite to eat. Then, she would call to check in and reassure them she was fine. But was she?

It had been three days, and Skylar found herself exhausted and feeling off. Maybe she should have stayed in the hospital like everyone said. She just couldn't get comfortable, slight twinges and pain seem to radiate from her hips. What was this continual thirst? Was this normal for being three months along in her pregnancy? She couldn't go on like this much longer. Something was seriously wrong with her or the baby. It was time to stop and find a doctor before things got any worse. As the day progressed, she was starting to get worried.

Looking to the side of the road, a sign came into view: Orlando, Florida. Funny, she hadn't known in which direction she had been traveling, just down the coast. It would be a nice place to visit, or stay for a bit. If nothing else, maybe she would see some of the things she dreamed of as a child.

While driving, she came upon an older hotel, which had seen better days. Right now, one was as good as the next. Going to the office, she found they rented rooms by the day, week, or month. This would do until she got herself on her feet again. Skylar didn't feel like running around to find anything else.

Skylar had asked the manager for a phone book; she wanted to find a doctor, not go to the ER. There was one not far from the hotel. Calling, she made an appointment for the following Monday with a Dr. Roberts.

With the things running through her mind, she couldn't wait to see this doctor. Would they both be all right? She hoped so.

By Sunday, Skylar was impatient for the time of her appointment. It seemed like the day was dragging. The nurse had said she was lucky to get an appointment, as the doctor had no other openings. But it was hard to wait until the afternoon. It was getting harder to think as the day wore on. Had a cloud moved through her thoughts? Maybe she should call home and talk with Jean for a few minutes, then get some sleep.

Finally, it was time for her to leave for her appointment. Upon arriving, she informed the receptionist, "I'm Skylar Evans. I've got a four o'clock appointment."

Ten minutes later, the nurse called her name. "Skylar Evans? This way please. Relax, you seem nervous. I promise I've not lost a patient, yet, during this part of the visit."

Skylar chuckled, feeling some of the tension leave. The nurse checked over and finished filling out the forms. After all the initial checks, the nurse had Skylar follow her to an exam room to wait for the doctor. While waiting, Skylar felt somewhat on the strange side, so she didn't notice the doctor coming in.

"Are you alright?" Dr. Roberts asked.

"I don't know. I feel very strange. It's all coming and going." Skylar didn't know how to explain what she was feeling.

"Let's get you examined, then I want to run some tests." Dr. Roberts was concerned by what he was seeing. All the bruising, he needed to find out what had gone on. Get her away from whomever had done this. "Ms. Evans, I need to question you about your injuries."

Things came back into focus, and Skylar told the doctor what had happened to her.

"Get dressed. I'm going to have a nurse bring you to my office to talk and make some decisions about your condition."

After dressing, the nurse took her to the office.

Skylar tried to imagine what was coming. "Doctor?"

"Ms. Evans, let me get right to the point. I'm not one to beat around the bush. I don't like what I'm seeing. You need additional tests run. It could be something as simple as your sugar levels being low, or it could be something from the beating you received.

First, we need to run a complete blood analysis, and then do a sonogram to see if any other injuries show up that you weren't aware of. We'll go from there and see if anything else needs scheduled. If possible, I'd like them done today."

"Does it all have to be done today, right now?" Skylar was scared.

"We need to see what is going on, if you want to get yourself on track." His phone buzzed then, which gave Skylar a moment to think.

"I guess you're right." She answered when Dr. Roberts had silenced his phone.

"Good, I'll get it all arranged. "One of my nurses is going with you. I'll put a rush on the results, also. Hopefully, we can go over some of the tests before the day is over."

Skylar looked at the doctor. "But it's already going on five o'clock."

"It's fine. Hours are till eight. Now go gather up your things and the nurse will be out in a minute."

"Okay, will everything be –" Skylar stammered.

"We'll wait and see what the tests show. Don't go borrowing trouble." The doctor motioned for the nurse to come inside. "You go with Ms. Evans. I believe there is more wrong with this young lady than she realizes. She may need someone with her for moral support."

"Yes doctor."

★★★

Most of the testing was done. Skylar was laying on a table, watching a little spot the technician had pointed out. Was that her baby there on the monitor? She wished Rhys was there, so he could be sharing this time.

As she lay there imagining what their baby was going to look like when it was born, she realized it was going to be a long six months. The waiting was going to be the hardest to endure while alone.

When the technician finished, they sent her back up to see the doctor. Would the nurse tell her anything, if she asked? Probably not.

Dr. Roberts confirmed she was starting her fourth month, and her due date should be around February 28th. "We need to talk seriously about what these tests showed."

He was worried about the other spots on the sonogram. They could be a number of things.

It could be a part of a damaged fetus, multiple births, or something unrelated. This woman showed how much she wanted this baby, but she needed to understand it might not be possible.

It was late when Skylar got back to her apartment. There were so many things to think about, especially the decision the doctor said she had to think over. What would the other tests show, if anything? Making herself a cup of tea, taking it out on the balcony, she called Jean to talk and tell her about the tests.

What a sad situation this was. And it was all because of John and the injuries he had given her. She was fighting to save the very life of her child. The baby was still at stake due to him, even though he wasn't anywhere near. How bizarre was that?

The beating had done more damage than they first thought. Dr. Roberts said she needed to have an operation desperately. She was feeling strange once again, and it was time to go back inside and lay down. What was it he said, why couldn't she remember?

Skylar fell into a restless sleep. When she woke, she was thinking on her dilemma. The operation was the only way to save their lives. Wasn't it? No, he said the best she could do was terminate this pregnancy so they could get on with saving her life. Didn't they know, she would have no life if the baby was gone?

Finally, she remembered it was a pelvic fracture and a small uterine rupture. If she didn't choose the operation, they both would probably die. With this being the only link to Rhys, there was no choice. How would she be able to face all the tomorrows? He said there was a thirty percent chance the baby would make it if they operated, but it might not be alright, if it lived. And he wasn't sure she could even carry to full term.

On Thursday, Skylar felt worse than ever. She couldn't think of what she was supposed to be doing. Did it matter? She didn't care if she ever got out of bed again. In a lucid moment, the thought of John accomplishing what he set out to do terrified her. She wouldn't let him destroy everything.

But she found she was too sick to get out of bed, and couldn't even remember important information. What day was it? Needing to know the date, she realized she may have left it too late. She slumped back against the pillows, unable to help herself. By morning, or soon after, she would probably be dead.

Jean and Harry were worried. They hadn't talked with Skylar since after her appointment. She wasn't picking up her phone.

CHAPTER 24

RHYS BEGAN TO PULL HIMSELF out of his guilt-ridden grief after a couple weeks of torture. Realizing things were over in his old life, he decided that today was literally going to be the first day of the rest of his life.

The talk he had wanted to have with Skylar was overdue by about a week. Thinking back on all he had intended to do, and how it all went wrong, he realized he would let nothing come between them if he could help it.

Rhys checked around the ranch, but couldn't find her. Where was she? He had been holed up in the library, but certainly she hadn't left?

He went in search of his family, or had they gone back to their homes after the service? Someone at the ranch was bound to know where she was, though. The only person he found handy was the housekeeper, Sarah, so he asked her.

"Sarah, have you seen Skylar today?"

"No Rhys, I haven't. She's not here."

Rhys probed. "Where is she, in town shopping?"

Sarah felt guilty due to her nephew, but she was angry with Rhys also. "No! She left shortly after the services."

Rhys didn't believe it. "You mean to tell me, she's gone off by herself?"

Sarah was shaking her head. "She went with Mr. Landon. And I hate to say this, no one has heard from her since."

Rhys had never been so angry. "She's gone, and no one felt the need to tell me she was going? She's been gone what, three days? Dammit to hell, why wasn't I told?"

"Rhys, no one could reach you. You were here, but weren't. It has been over two weeks, not three days. The boys have been taking turns coming to stay every couple of days to make sure you weren't alone. Your grandfather couldn't even get through to you."

Rhys was floored. He had lost two weeks. "Son-of-a-bitch, that's just an excuse."

Sarah raised her eyebrow at him. "Is it?"

Skylar left without saying anything to him. Or had she? If he had been out of it, would he remember? Or was she like Bree after all? She played the part real well. When would he learn not to trust with his heart?

He had to get out of the house.

He had no idea in which direction he had walked. He thought maybe he should just head back to work, and bury himself in it like the last time. But this time, he was so sure. Was it his fault? When was the last time he talked with her?

Sarah went in search of Alan and told him what had occurred. Alan figured he knew what Rhys was thinking, the wrong things probably. He had to stop him. Rhys had to know the truth before he was sorry. Alan found him at the pond, "Rhys?"

"Not now, Alan," Rhys said with anger.

Alan continued. "Rhys, I know why you're out here. We need to talk about Skylar."

"What the hell is there to talk about? I picked another winner there, didn't I?" Rhys's sarcasm was coming through.

"Rhys, pull your head out of your ass for a minute. You're wrong, you know. *You* checked out on her. You didn't keep her in it." Alan said.

"Sure, and she couldn't wait to leave either. Tell me another one. Just leave me the hell alone." Rhys went to walk off from this conversation. He didn't need it, and wasn't ready for anymore now.

Alan grabbed his arm. "Rhys, you dumb shit. You will listen a minute. It isn't how you think it is. And she left a letter for you as well."

"Big of her, wasn't it!" Rhys sneered.

Alan was shouting now. "Dammit Rhys!! You know in your heart she wasn't like Bree."

At Rhys's surprised look, Alan knew he'd hit the nail on the head. So he went on talking. "The letter should explain the whys of her actions. If it's any comfort, she was suffering just as much as you, if not more. She lost a sister she never knew, and you pulled away. She felt leaving was the only door open for her."

"That's shit and you know it," Rhys shouted back.

Alan was using the raised eyebrow Sarah had used earlier. "Is it, Rhys?"

"Yes, I wouldn't have left." Knowing it was a lie, he couldn't finish the statement.

"Didn't you in a way?" Alan asked straight forwardly.

"I guess I did," he said reluctantly. "That's why I shut up." Rhys sighed. "I hadn't meant for her to leave though. Things were so crazy. Wish one of you would have just kick me in the ass to wake me up."

"Rhys, no one is a mind reader," Alan said while patting his brother on the back.

"Dammit," Rhys quietly said.

"Come on, let's go up to the house. Just be glad it was my turn to be here. One of the others would probably have kicked your ass for being a fool," Alan laughed.

★★★

"I've been tempted to read this letter, so I could help when the time came, but I figured whatever is in it is between the two of you. She asked me to keep it safe until you thought about her," Alan said while holding the envelope out to Rhys. "You'll want to read in private. Before I go, know she struggled long and hard making the decision she did," Alan spoke somberly.

Rhys still had some anger. "Yeah, so long she was gone right after the services for her sister."

Alan shook his head. "Don't judge her harshly. It started with what she overheard the day we brought her home from the hospital."

Rhys didn't understand. "What's it got to do with anything?"

"Rhys, Rhys, Rhys. You don't remember? You were talking to Grandfather about Bree and your life. What it would've been like if John hadn't killed her."

Rhys was stymied; she had heard what was said? "When we were talking, I didn't mean it the way it sounded, it was all a waste. Her life and the child's. Then it could have been Skylar also. I kind of turned into myself."

"Right, you pushed her away." Alan was still holding the letter out to his brother. When he didn't take it, he placed it in his hands.

Rhys stood there staring at the letter. Would it help in finding her, or was it a Dear John letter to get him and his family out of her life? They had brought nothing but trouble to her, how much did she hate them? Should he burn it and be done, forget she existed? How could he when she was his other half?

Throwing it on the desk, he walked over to stare out of the window. He stood at this very window when he saw her trying to walk off, after their first true encounter. He went and brought her back. Had it been a sign?

Running his hands through his hair, he exhaled the breath he hadn't known he was holding. He was getting old and tired. He knew in his heart she wasn't like Bree, except in looks. She was a strong and caring person, and she proved how honest she was right from the start.

To his knowledge, she had never lied to him. She always told him the truth, whether he wanted to hear it or not, always saying what she thought. He was remembering her as she truly was, not how he had been thinking earlier. She didn't throw curves at you; she shot straight from the hip in her dealings.

She had endured so much for him and from him. Even while they had been strangers. Right from the start it was as though they belonged. How could he have forgotten what they felt? Only thinking of himself, these last few days…weeks.

It was finally sinking in, and going over to the desk, he sat. Picking the letter up, he turned it over and over. He was stalling; did he deserve what was written? Would it be a good thing, or was it over? He told himself … *Open it already.*

Knowing he had ignored her since the attack, he felt guilty beyond belief He had been afraid because his family – no correction – a so-called member of the family, had hurt her. He didn't give her a chance to say if she wanted to be part of this family, and he took the choice from her by being an ass.

Should he read it, or leave her go without a fight?

Dammit, NO. She was his and he needed to know what she had been thinking the last night she had been at the ranch. He would then find out where she was and bring her home with the family who loved her.

Finally, opening it, he unfolded the sheets. They seemed to be stained with what could only have been tears. Closing his eyes, he swallowed the lump in his throat. Dammit, he was a bastard for making her cry. Pulling himself together, he began to read what would either make or break him.

CHAPTER 25

July 22, 2015

My Dearest Rhys,

IF YOU'RE READING THIS AT *last, then I know you were thinking of me. I hope and pray you're having good thoughts, and not ones of hate and disgust. I know your temper, and would like for you to read the letter in its entirety before discarding it as a lie. You see, I know how you think. I tell you truthfully it had to be this way.*

I want you to know, you will always be in my thoughts and dreams. Whether we end up together or not, my love will be with you for eternity. I promise you, I will be thinking of you often. They will be good thoughts, as there can be no other kind where you are concerned.

There was a reason why I left without saying good-bye. See, I knew it would be the first thing you'd want to know. It was because I couldn't bring myself to say it. If I would've faced you, I probably wouldn't have left. If you look at it one way, I was a coward in the end. I was afraid to look into your eyes, in case there would be indifference in them. After hearing you talk with your grandfather, and the way we were with each other in your room, I just didn't know what to think about our relationship.

So I left this letter to be given to you, only when and IF you asked about me. It was the only way I could see to handle it. I realize the love you had for Bree was still there to a point. It had never been resolved. You needed to work out those feelings on your own, it seemed. And I do understand it. I also had things to work out myself.

It seemed you were trying to, and seceded in, shutting me out. You made me feel you wanted to deal with it on your own with no help from me. What was I to do, but let you do it your way?

This is why I figured it was a good time to work out my own life. Finding out Matt was my father and coming face to face with him, was disconcerting to say the least. And the fact I had a sister, it was a bit much for me to deal with. On top of everything, I had the need to feel some peace.

Realizing my sister and I ended up loving the same man, but years apart. Well, just one more thing to think about. There has to be something about you, which drew us both to you. I really believe Bree loved you when she died. Everyone says she was happy then.

While in John's power, I was fighting for my life. My mind was racing with thoughts of what if. Like, if Bree had lived, would we have met? Could we have been close, maybe friends, or just sisters due to the blood we shared? It was funny, our paths crossing at this time in both of our lives. It had to be destiny. I was wondering if I would have ever met you or your family otherwise.

Whatever, I'm glad I had the chance to know all of you as we did. Even if it was for a brief period of time. This is a memory I'll be able to take with me wherever I am or whatever I'm doing. It will help me get through the days ahead of me.

I have to be thankful for at least the memories. I'll have them always, even if I can't have you. Let me say this again, and it will never have been said enough: I'm so very glad we met. Don't ever think I regret the day we met, however unorthodox it was at Sam's Place. What a way to get a girl to go with you.

The night before the memorial service for Bree, I realized something when you came to bed. There was a gulf forming, with no bridge for me to get over. I knew then, you didn't need me around complicating your life. I had thought you were going to need me to get through it all, but I was wrong. You never seem to need anyone, and I felt like a disruption in your life. Something you didn't want or need then or maybe at any other time.

I'm sorry I'm rambling. There's just so much going through my mind.

Please believe, I think this was the best thing for both of us. Don't think I suddenly went crazy after everything. I write this in a rational state of mind. It's my hope I remember it all, and don't forget something before I think I'm done with this letter. This was the hardest decision of my life, but I felt it was the only decision I could make for all concerned. The only one that made sense to me.

I left Alan under the impression I'd be with Matt. I won't be, though. I'm not ready to call him my father. Don't be angry with your brother. He isn't responsible for my actions. But I knew, or doubted, is a better word, he would've ever let me leave the ranch if he had known my plans. Don't ask Matt where I am, because he won't know in the end either.

If, and when, I'm ready to see you again, I'll get in contact with you. Until this time comes, please respect I also need time. Neither of us have an easy road ahead of us.

Until we meet again, I'll not be a whole person. And the reason being, I leave you with my heart. Please cherish it while it's in your keeping. Don't destroy it.

I have only one regret. Well, that's not entirely true. The one uppermost in my mind is I didn't have a small piece of your heart to carry with me. It would have been something to keep me going in the days ahead. I could have brought it out when I most needed it, taking the love it would generate to heal me.

I love you more than words can say.

I want to leave you with one more thought before I close this letter. Don't hate John. He was a very sick person. And help Sarah deal with it all. You saw firsthand what hate did to him, it ate at his soul for so many years. Hate is destructive, because it does no one any good. All it does is destroy the person, and I don't want that for you.

I've found the forgiveness in my heart for him. I'll never forget the horror of what he put me through, or of my own past, or what he caused each of us to lose. Don't let him take anymore from you. Try and think back to the hate you felt for Bree. Did it do any good? I don't think so! Remember, it won't be any different this time either.

Love is the most precious gift in this world. You should not only give it to another, but share it. It's something I can't explain; you must realize it yourself. Sharing seems to be the hardest thing in the world for most people to do.

Never doubt, I love you with my whole heart, and I think I shared it buy trusting you enough to leave it in your keeping. You know, I trust no other as I do you.

I'll love you forever,
Skylar Evans

P.S.
I must find the real Skylar again. It seems as though she became lost in the last few weeks. Something you warned me of. It's time to go back to the very beginning for me. Only then will I be able to start this healing process.

THINK OF ME OFTEN, WILL YOU?

★★★

Rhys couldn't believe what he read. The range of emotions it brought out in him, she hit them all. What should he do?

CHAPTER 26

WHERE COULD SHE BE? WHERE had his head been, to try and keep her at arm's length to save her from his feelings? Shaking his head, he pondered what he had read. What clues where there to help him? He reread the letter, over and over, until he knew it by heart. Had she written anything between the lines? No, she always said what she thought. What were the loudest points she tried to get across?

Why would she think herself a coward. Where in the hell could she get an idea like this? She faced everything thrown at her head on, and she was a fighter, not a quitter. She had to know he loved her, no one else. He never felt this kind of emotion for another living soul.

Why hadn't she understood what he felt after finding the bodies, was guilt for letting John get close enough to harm them? And he hadn't even managed to keep her safe from John's madness. He guessed he didn't give her a chance to understand.

He had thought he had loved Bree, but it wasn't anything like what he felt for Skylar. He didn't stop and think because what he had with Skylar was all-consuming. Not only was his heart involved, his mind and soul where also. She was his other half, the better half. If she was gone, he may as well be, too.

What she said was true, he had drawn into himself, shutting everyone else out. What a fool he was. The old saying about hindsight was true. You can't go back and change things; you have to go on from the present with your life.

Even if Bree had lived, Rhys doubted they would still be together. All he could think of at this moment was that he wasn't about to have a life without Skylar. He would find her and make her believe in their love, so they could be together.

While heading to his car, Rhys pulled his phone out to call the pilot and get everything ready for take-off.

If he had anything to do with it, things were going to be right this time around. She was his, and by damn if he wouldn't prove it to her once and for all. Memories weren't enough for him, not with this one. He needed the real thing in his life. His mind raced the whole trip.

A car was waiting when the plane landed, and he headed into town. Would she be here? It wasn't to be.

"May I help you sir?" The manager of her apartment building asked.

"I'm looking for Ms. Evans," Rhys stated.

"I'm sorry, sir, but she isn't in right now," the manager told him.

Rhys was getting impatient. "When do you expect her back?"

"I can't give you this information." The manager said wondering if he should buzz for help with this guy.

Rhys was angry, damn the man. Taking a deep breath, he tried another way. "I understand you are doing your job. But this is important. She is to be my wife, but we had a misunderstanding."

"Sir, I'm sorry. I honestly don't have the information. Ms. Evans just asked for her mail be held, and she would either send for it or pick it up at a later date."

"What the hell do you mean?" Rhys shouted.

"Sir, please. I have to ask you leave now before I call for help. I won't ask again."

Rhys turned and left. He hadn't found out squat. Taking out the letter again, he read it over. What had he missed before? *Skylar, if you only knew how much of my heart you did take with you.*

Rhys realized there was something else she was going to be dealing with on her own for now. She was carrying their child, with no help around. Did she yet know she was pregnant? She had to know by now.

What a jerk he had been. He wished she would know he needed her more than he ever needed anyone before. Dammit, why didn't he see it before? When she said she needed to go to the beginning, she meant back to where she came from. It had to be where she had lived before coming to Altoona because nothing else made any sense. What was it she had said? She had to find the real Skylar again.

Where was this place, why couldn't he think of it? It was there, but not there. His mind was putting him in a spin. What was the place she worked before, her boss's name? If he could remember those, then he would have them checked out. Be able to find her. Damn, why was he still drawing a blank in his head?

Starting his car, he drove across town, and where do you think he found himself? In front of Sam's Place, where it all began. Going in, he got a cup of coffee. Would he grasp any answers sitting here?

Losing himself in thought, he was stumped. All of a sudden, the name of the Blackwells seemed to jump in his head. Then it all came rushing back to him. That's it, things were looking up. Throwing money on the table, Rhys went rushing out to his car. He was off to Skylar's beginnings, Maple Grove, Pennsylvania.

When Rhys reached what he thought to be his destination, it was to find himself sitting in front of a beautiful brownstone house. It was funny, he was sitting there trying to get up his nerve to go and knock on the door. He never had this problem before. He was afraid of what he was going to find, or not find.

Taking a deep breath, he approached the house, and knocked. A woman answered the door and spoke to him. "May I help you?"

"I don't know. Could you tell me if this is the residence of Harry and Jean Blackwell? And if it is, then yes, you could help me," Rhys asked hesitantly.

"Well young man, apparently you have me at a disadvantage. You seem to know who we are, but we don't know you. My guess would be you had better come in and explain yourself to my husband and me. Then we'll take it from there and see if we can be of assistance to you."

Backing up, Jean let Rhys into the house. The woman, who he took to be Jean, motioned for him to follow her. They entered what had to be the living room, and that's when he came face to face with Matt Landon again.

Rhys was furious with Matt, but kept himself in check. He was the one who had let Skylar take off when she still wasn't well. Nodding to the other man, who had to be Harry Blackwell, Rhys noticed the looks he was receiving from the unknown man.

"Sir, may I introduce myself? Rhys Cantrell. I see the name already brings recognition to your eyes."

"I figured out who you were when you walked in." Harry was scrutinizing the man before him, this person who had hurt his Skylar so much. How, why, and what had brought him here on the heels of her real father? What exactly did he think to gain by coming here to them?

"The name confirmed who I thought you were." Motioning at Matt, then him, Harry went on. "As you're both obviously here for the same reasons, let me save you both some time." He sat heavily in a chair and glared at the men still standing.

"When Skylar came home to us, it was as if seeing a battered child all over again. And I'll tell you both something else, we didn't like it one damn bit," Harry spouted. Seeing both men were about to argue the point, Harry held up his hand to stay them from talking. "I'll be honest with you, she left here yesterday. There were still things she felt she had to deal with on her own. She needed to find somewhere peaceful, with no distractions or memories, to rest and heal physically, as well as mentally."

It seemed Harry hadn't even got the last word out, when Matt started. "Well, where did she go? She wasn't as well as she should have been when we left the ranch. I waited, to give her time with the two of you. I had every intention of coming and getting her. I feel she needed more medical attention, which if I had to, I was going to force her to get," Matt said with a huff.

Rhys hadn't known she was still ill. As it sunk in, Rhys rounded on Matt. "What the hell do you mean, she wasn't well yet? Just what kind of medical attention does she still need? Alan would never have let her leave the ranch if she was still hurt."

"Gentlemen, please! And I am using the term gentlemen very loosely. Kindly remember you are in my home here. And I will not tolerate this kind of behavior any longer," Jean said, and then went on.

"I grant she wasn't in the best of health, but what do either of you expect after everything she had been through. I'll tell you this, she was going to seek out a doctor for herself as soon as she got where she was going. I had her make me this promise. It was the only way I would have let her leave here. If I hadn't got the promise, she would be sitting here, you better to believe me," Jean finished.

"But where is she? You have to know. Surely you have an idea where she was heading. There has to be some clue." Rhys wondered. "You wouldn't have just let her disappear, or would you?" Rhys ranted at them.

"Now you hold on there. You don't know anything about shit. What kind of people are you used to dealing with in your life to act this way?" Harry shouted right back at Rhys.

"Listen Mr. Blackwell, I apologize for my outburst. But you have to understand, she means the world to me. She is my whole life, and without her, I may as well give up."

The Blackwells didn't know what to think. Was this young man sincere about his feelings for their girl? Or was it all just a show, so he could find out whether she was carrying his child? Just what kind of man was he, was the question.

Skylar had said she didn't think Rhys knew about the baby. She wanted Rhys to love her for herself, not the child she was carrying. How could they be sure of what his intentions were?

What should they do? Could they trust these two men not to hurt her anymore? The other option was, could they afford not to trust them? It was true, she hadn't been as well as she should.

Jean had an idea on how they could gauge these two men. She needed to know exactly what they knew. "Harry, let me ask them a few things."

Harry wasn't sure. "I hope you know what you're doing."

"It's the only way to be sure if we're doing the right thing for her," Jean said quietly.

"Alright!" Harry gave in.

Jean turned to the others. "Do either of you know how much Skylar had to deal with in her life?"

Both looked at her and answered without reservations. "Yes."

"Then she did talk with you, but I wonder how much."

Rhys was seeing red; this woman was wasting time he felt they didn't have. He felt as though Skylar was calling him for help. And he didn't want to fail her this time around. "Dammit, woman, if you don't tell me where she is – I have to find her, now. You may not believe this, but I feel there is something wrong. I have to get to her and make her see I love her with everything in me: mind, body, and soul. Most of all, I love her with my whole heart. I have to do this before it's too late, please." Rhys had tears close to the edge.

"Why didn't you speak of this before? It could have saved us some time, and both of you much pain," Jean answered.

"I would've, if Matt hadn't showed up at the ranch when he did. More than likely she would be my wife right now. I was going to ask her to marry me the night he got there. When it all sort of went crazy all around us. We couldn't get together for a talk or anything. Don't you understand, seeing him, caused her untold anguish. She had this picture she kept in her wallet. It was of her mother and a guy who had to be her father. That man is Matt." Rhys was talking, just to talk, having no idea that he'd said the one thing in this world that would make the Blackwells believe in him.

Harry was stunned by what he was hearing Rhys speak of. "You saw the picture? I never dreamed she would show anyone, let alone talk about it."

Matt spoke up then. "You mean you didn't realize that I was her father?"

"No ... I mean, yes, we know. But for her to share something personal, that's a big step. It means she trusted Rhys enough for him to know her past," Jean said.

"You can see how close we had become by this time. She shared a great many things. More than anyone could know. She told me her life story, how much both of you mean to her. You did so much for her. Because of you and your love she stayed a whole person. I would say we're very close, so much so, she's carrying my child right now. We created a miracle, a new life." Rhys felt so lost, but still clung to the hope that the Blackwells could help him find Skylar in time to save her.

With tears in her eyes, Jean turned to her husband. "Harry, I think we should tell them what we know."

"You're right, Jean." Harry turned to Rhys and Matt, and shrugged. "She was heading down the coast toward Florida. It seems she always wanted to go there. She promised to call every other day to check in.

By the time she calls today, you could be partway down there. Besides, she will give us the address once she's settled."

"Florida, that's all you have? Dammit, what if she – "Rhys ran his hand through his hair. "Once again I must ask your pardon. I feel so frustrated, not knowing much of anything. I thank you for what you have given us. It is more than we had before."

"You will call later." Jean said as a statement, not a question.

They exchanged cell numbers. "You can be sure I'll keep in touch. I don't want you wondering about her. If she says where she is when she calls, let me know immediately." Rhys answered.

"We will son. All we can say is good luck."

CHAPTER 27

SO THE SEARCH WOULD START, and the story was going to have a different ending this time. Rhys knew it in his heart, they would be together again. Something kept telling him things would work out.

Rhys had kept in touch with the Blackwells since his visit. Skylar hadn't given them an address as of yet. He felt like he was going to lose his sanity if something didn't give soon. He hired some private detectives, so all he could do was wait. He wanted to be doing this himself, but it was better to leave it to the professionals.

Rhys was on edge, ready to fall either way. The feelings he had about Skylar needing him had grown out of proportion. It seemed like she was calling out to him in desperation. He felt they were connected through their souls. Did she feel it? Skylar had to know he would be searching for her, didn't she? All he could do was hope. Rhys kept looking at the calendar. How long would it be before he heard something?

On the morning of August 25th, a call came into Rhys's office. It was from one of the private detectives who was working on Skylar's case.

Rhys had been staring off into space. He should be in Florida, helping to find her; it would be more than he was accomplishing here. His intercom buzzed. "Yes, what is it Mrs. Straw?"

"There's a call on line one. It's from one of the detectives. He said to tell you he's found her." Not giving his secretary time to speak, Rhys cut the connection to the intercom and was punching the button for line one.

He spoke loud enough while he was picking up the receiver for the party to hear him. "Rhys Cantrell speaking. What have you got?"

"Sir, we traced her to Florida, just like you said," the investigator said.

"Dammit man, I knew where she was going. Tell me something I don't know." Rhys answered a little louder than normal.

The investigator continued, "Sorry sir. What gave us the edge, was telling us to check with different doctors. I won't go into the details on how I got the information."

Rhys felt like ringing the guy's neck. "Alright man, get to the point. Either you know where she is or you're wasting my time with this call." His voice raised another notch by the end.

This man had worked for Rhys before. By the tone of his voice, he knew not to play around any longer. "Right! Well, she's rented an apartment in Orlando. The address is 927 Lakewood Avenue. I better warn you before you hotfoot it down here, you're not going to like the location of this place one bit."

Finally, Rhys thought. Rhys sighed with relief, not realizing he had been holding his breath. "I'll deal with it when I get there. Don't worry about it any longer."

"Is there anything else you want us to do for you?" The investigator asked.

"No that's it. Thanks isn't enough to say how I'm feeling. You can expect a bonus with your check," Rhys answered.

"Thank you, sir. Goodbye."

Rhys thought he was going to see Skylar soon. There were many things to arrange so he could leave. He phoned the pilot to get everything ready so they would take off immediately upon his arriving.

He phoned the Blackwells to let them know he was going to bring Skylar home soon. Then he phoned Matt, and told him where he was headed. "I'm asking you because you are her father, do you want to go along? If so, be at the airport in one hour. There will be no waiting on you if you're late. The plane will leave when I'm on board. Remember that!"

Matt felt emotional. "Thanks for calling. I'll be there soon. I've a lot to make up for with both of you. I feel as though she is calling us."

Rhys knew what he meant; he felt it too. "I know, I've felt it. Enough of this talk, I have things that need taken care of. If I see you, then I see you." Breaking the connection, he phoned his father's number. "Dad."

"Rhys, good to hear from you son. Wait, I can hear something in your voice. You've had news, haven't you?" Brandon was excited.

"As a matter of fact, I do have news. They've found where she's staying. I have the address. I'm on my way. I just wanted to let you know first," Rhys said with happiness.

"Thanks, son. I'll let the rest of the family know what's going on. Want me to call and get things going at the airport for you?"

"Already done."

"Fine then, you head out and I'll arrange things in the Orlando airport. I'll come to the office and take care of anything needing done. And son, good luck." Brandon felt some relief for his son.

"Thanks, Dad. I may need some luck with this one." Rhys hung up. Grabbing a bag on the way would be no problem. His place was nearby, and he had kept a bag packed for just this reason. Rhys was thinking, would he have left without Matt? He doubted it.

Rhys arrived at the airport to find Matt waiting on him. They nodded to one another, then boarded the plane. Each remained silent during the flight, both hoping for the best.

★★★

"Sir, are you Rhys Cantrell?"

"Yes, I don't have time to talk with you now," Rhys stated.

"No sir, you don't understand. I have a car for you. Your father arranged it. The directions to your destination are in this folder," the man said while handing the folder and keys off to Rhys.

"Thanks." Rhys took the keys and nodded to Matt to get in. They were heading out to find Skylar. After reaching the street they had been searching for, they went slow trying to find the correct house number. They were almost to the end of the street, when they saw what had to be the oldest hotel in use.

"Well, I think this is it," Matt stated simply, not liking the look of the place.

Rhys looked at the building. They had been right; he hated where he was finding her. This couldn't be right. They had to make a mistake with the address. The only way to find out for sure was to go and ask. He would have to hold her until his anger faded. Because right now, he wanted to wring her neck for staying in a place like this.

Matt was tired of waiting for Rhys to move. It was time to interrupt Rhys's thoughts and find his daughter. "Let's go. I hate the thought she might be in there as much as you do. So the sooner we go in, the sooner we'll have her out of there."

Throwing the door open, Rhys spoke angrily. "Not dammed soon enough, as far as I'm concerned."

Leading the way, Rhys bounded up the steps and knocked on the first door he came to. Waiting for his knock to be answered, he looked around. The inside wasn't as bad as the outside.

An elderly woman answered the door. "What do you want?"

"Would you happen to know if Skylar Evans is in residence? If she is, I'd like to know which room is hers."

The woman looked concerned, and worried. "I'm not saying she is, and I'm not saying she isn't. What do you want to know for?"

"Listen, we have to find her before it is too late," Rhys demanded.

"I don't like this one bit. Some other men were here a few days ago, asking about her, too. What's she done since you all looking for her?" The woman asked.

"She hasn't done anything; this is personal. Now will you tell us what you know?" Rhys was getting frustrated, it was like pulling teeth.

"Is she in some sort of trouble? You can't be too careful now days," she deadpanned.

Rhys was getting mad as hell. "Listen lady, I can assure you there is no trouble. At least not the kind you seem to mean. We are worried about her. Okay? Let me tell you something. If I don't get some answers quickly, I may just have to start going room to room until I find her."

Matt touched Rhys's arm. "This isn't getting us anywhere, fighting with this woman."

"You stay out of it!" Stepping aside, Rhys let the woman get a look at Matt. "This is her father, and I use that term loosely, and I'm her fiancé. UNDERSTAND? A misunderstanding took place, and she left before it could be dealt with. I'd like to make amends with her now and take her back home."

"I don't know, if she ran away, then maybe she doesn't want to see either of you again. I saw her bruised all up. And besides, I don't much care for being screamed at."

"I apologize for my manners, but we have to find her. And it wasn't us who hurt her like you think. She was hurt in an accident, and wasn't completely well when she left. I'm afraid she might have gotten worse being here on her own. Dammit, we're at our wit's end to find her before it is too late."

Looking them over, she saw the tears in Rhys's eyes. Knowing in her heart, they were sincere, they weren't there to hurt this girl more, she conceded, "Very well. I'm convinced you're who you say you are. She is staying here, and I've been worried about her."

"Fine, what room?" Then it sunk in what else she said. More concerned than ever, he asked, "Why, what's wrong with her?"

The woman hesitated. "Well, to be truthful, she hasn't been out of her room in about three days. I think she might've been ill, but didn't want to seem nosey if she was staying in for no reason."

Rhys wanted to shout at this point, then thought better of it. "Where in the hell is the room she's in?"

"Next floor up, second door on the right." Rhys turned to go, but paused as she spoke again.

"Wait."

"What is it now?" Rhys said with impatience. It seemed as though they had been talking for hours, but it had only been minutes.

"You'll probably need a pass key if she is sick and can't answer the door."

"Well, hurry up for God's sake," Rhys shouted with uncontrolled anger

Slipping back into her room, she returned a few moments later and handed the key to them. As soon as the key touched Rhys's hand, he was off like a shot. He took the stairs two at a time. Upon reaching the door he was searching for, he didn't pause to knock. Without hesitation, putting the key into the lock, he proceeded to open the door.

Pushing it open, Rhys saw her almost at once. He stopped and looked over at her. Closing his eyes for a moment, he thought. Was this real or another dream of finding her? Then he heard a moan, which brought him out of his wondering. In but a few strides, he crossed the room to the bed. Reaching out, he was afraid to touch her; she looked pale and fragile.

With the thought in mind, he gathered his courage up, and touched her. She was burning up with fever. Matt had reached the room and stopped him in his tracks. She looked pale enough to be a ghost, and he was shocked to the core. Afraid to ask the question, but more afraid not to ask, he breathed, "Is she —?"

"Not yet, but she needs help. Call 911 now," Rhys shouted.

"My God, what's wrong with her?" Matt stammered out.

"Dammit Matt, we don't have time for a discussion on her condition. I said she needs help." Seeing the lady at the door, he spoke to her in a forceful tone. "Lady, call the closest hospital and tell them we're on our way with a very sick patient. They better have the best damn doctor on staff waiting for us."

The lady didn't question the orders, but turned and went to do his bidding.

"Matt, we can't wait on the ambulance. We'll take her ourselves. I'm going to get her ready, find out from the lady where the hospital is." Rhys said with emotion.

"Yeah." Matt had no words.

Rhys lifted Skylar from the bed, making sure the sheet was around her. Turning, he found Matt was still standing there. "Dammit Matt, snap out of it! She needs us to get things started now, not next week. So move, man, move!"

Matt was startled out of his stupor, and turning, he went to do what should have been done already. Matt felt old and tired suddenly. He had failed Bree, now he was failing Skylar.

Giving in, and letting her do what she wanted, might just be the cause of her death. And it would be his fault. Matt exited the building as Rhys was putting Skylar into the backseat, then climbed in himself. As Matt approached the car, he saw Rhys cradling Skylar in his arms. It seemed as though he was trying to will her to hold on.

Crawling into the driver's seat, Matt followed the directions the woman gave him. This kept his mind off of what was going on in the back. It took them close to twenty minutes to reach the hospital. Pulling in front of the emergency room door, Rhys threw the door open and rushed into the hospital.

The head nurse saw him come in; it looked like he was holding a young woman for all he was worth. She knew immediately she had better take charge of the situation. This had to be the patient they were waiting on. "Bring her this way, please."

The nurse led the way into one of the ER rooms. Walking over to the bed, she motioned for the man to lay his charge down. When he didn't, she spoke, "Please put her on the table, sir. We can't very well see what's wrong with her if you won't let her go."

Rhys realized what the nurse meant, but laying her down was the hardest thing for him to do. He turned to the nurse. "I think you should be aware of a few facts. She – she was hurt recently. Actually, someone beat her. It wasn't long ago. It happened in the middle of July. She didn't stay in the hospital long enough, apparently."

Rhys looked at the nurse taking vital signs. It seemed as though she wasn't paying attention to what he said. "Listen nurse, did you hear anything I've said?" Rhys asked sarcastically with a raised eyebrow.

"Actually sir, I've heard every word," the nurse shot right back.

"Well how the hell was I to know? Anyway, she's been through a great deal lately, physically as well as emotionally," Rhys said through clenched teeth to keep from shouting.

"Yes, I can tell some of what you're saying." Maybe he would let her get on with her work now, since she talked back to him this time.

"She's carrying our child," Rhys sad in a choked voice, while he stood looking down on the love of his life.

"Fine sir. I'm going to ask you to step out of the room now. The doctor needs to do this without distraction." She had to get this guy out of the way so they could take care of the patient in the best way possible.

Rhys stood there, looking at the nurse. If she thought she was getting rid of him. She better think again. He had just found her, and he wanted to know exactly what was going on. No sir, not happening, he was staying.

Seeing he was making no move to leave, the nurse went around the table toward him. "I understand this is a difficult time, but you have to leave for now so we can do our job to the best of our ability. And if you're in the way, well, it will not help." She took a step, gently stepping him back out of the door.

"I promise to tell the doctor what you've told me. You know, you'll be helping her more by giving us the space we need. I know the desk is going to need the information about her, and you can give it. Do you think you could go and do it, while we see to her?"

Rhys knew it would be for the best if he did as the nurse asked, but it was hard to leave her now. "You will let me know?"

"As soon as we know anything, someone will come to you at once. And one other thing—" the nurse started to say.

"Yes, what is it?" Rhys answered in a vexed voice.

"If you would have let me finish, I was going to tell you to make sure you tell them at the desk the name of the other hospital. Tell them the doctor will be wanting her records on her stay for the accident. Then they'll contact that hospital's staff and we'll be able to get a clearer picture of what we're dealing with."

Rhys turned back, taking a last look at Skylar. It was time to do as the nurse had asked. Telling them everything he could think of, any scrap of information he could, he would do all in his power to get her the help she needed.

CHAPTER 28

IT SEEMED AS THOUGH HOURS had passed since they had brought Skylar into the hospital. Rhys and Matt sat, then paced, drinking cup after cup of coffee. "How much longer do you think we'll have to wait?" Matt said in a sad voice.

"They said as soon as they knew what they were dealing with, they would send someone to talk with us," Rhys said quietly.

He had to call the Blackwells and let them know what was happening, but that was not a call he was looking forward to. Going over to the doorway for some privacy, he placed his call.

Matt rounded on him, when he hung up. "Why the hell call them?"

Shaking his head, Rhys looked at this man. "They are her family, before me or you. Accept it and let it go."

"I didn't even get to go in with her to start with. But you made sure you were with her," Matt stated.

"Matt, don't start now. I think I caused enough problems with the nurse for the both of us. Someone will be out soon."

Matt knew he was being unreasonable. "I know, it's just this waiting's getting to me."

They began to pace again; the nurse on duty in the waiting room had seen many families almost wear holes in the floor waiting for news.

Each time they saw someone coming toward them, they thought they were going to get news of Skylar. They never stopped to talk. Both men were at the breaking point when Skylar was wheeled out towards the elevator. Both moved toward where she was. Evidently, they were admitting her.

As Rhys walked toward them, he knew he had to see her with his own eyes before believing anyone she was all right. When he was beside the bed, the nurse looked up to him and tried to step in front of him. "Sir?"

"You're not the same nurse. I have to see her, make sure she's alright. Before you take her wherever you are going." Rhys was choked up.

The first nurse came out. "It's alright Sue, he's with her."

Rhys took a breath. If he talked to her, would she be able to hear him? "I'm here baby, just hold on. Things are going to be fine."

The elevator arrived, and the nurse named Sue spoke. "Sir, we have to take her up now. We can't wait around for you to talk to her any longer."

Rhys sighed. "I understand. When will we know what we're up against?"

"You'll have to talk with the doctor," she told him as the doors closed.

Turning, he saw Matt had returned from getting more coffee. And it didn't look like he was too pleased. "I missed seeing her again, didn't I?"

"They're taking her upstairs," Rhys sighed.

With anger, Matt spoke louder than he should have. "You got to see her though, and I suppose you know what's going on with her, too."

"Matt, for God's sake. They brought her out, and I went over to check to see for myself if she was still... It looks bad though. And no, I don't know anything yet. The nurse said we have to talk to the doctor and find out how she is. We have to wait here, not even go up with her!" Rhys said with clenched teeth. He was tired of this fighting.

About ten minutes went by when the doctor came out and started toward them. Was he coming to talk with them, or was he going by like all the rest? Then, at what seemed like the last possible moment, he stopped by them and asked, "Are either of you gentlemen with the young lady named Skylar, who they just brought out to go upstairs?"

Matt stepped up to the doctor. "Yes, I'm her father and this is her fiancé', Rhys Cantrell."

"Fine, then you both need to take a seat. I'm Doctor Timms, and I have a few things to explain about Skylar's condition. Luckily, the doctor she saw a few days ago was a friend of mine. Her case bothered him a great deal, so we discussed what to do about her. He had described her, so I thought I recognized her. In my opinion, what he decided was the same course of action I would follow.

"Before you ask, yes, we are aware of the complications she is dealing with. She had told him about what happened, so he already had her file sent over from the other hospital and talked to the doctors. There was more damage from the beating than anyone first thought.

"I see by the look on your faces what you're thinking. You want to blame them, but don't. It wasn't apparent till recently, due to her pregnancy. You have to understand, her body is adjusting itself, and it's expanding on the inside right now for the baby. The expanding in fact, caused these injuries to show up now."

"But doctor?" Rhys wanted to know what was wrong.

"No, wait, let me finish. I want to explain how this came about. I have to be straight with you. She's a very ill woman. Her life is in immediate danger. Dr. Roberts told her this and gave her the options as to what could be done. They were under the impression they had a few weeks to let her make up her mind. That way she wouldn't feel pressured into making a hasty decision."

"Well, what happened to her few weeks to make these decisions?" Rhys asked the doctor, giving him that skeptical and terrifying look of his.

"As you know, apparently she didn't have the time. Her body is changing faster than anticipated. She needs the operation Dr. Roberts talked about with her. He'll be in soon to take over this case, as he is her current physician. He can fill in more of the details for you.

"For now, till he does get here, why don't you go up and see her? She was put in room 1408, and she is probably settled by now. I have to warn you, there are lots of tubes and monitors. It may look like a lot, but be assured they are necessary at this point."

Dr. Timms stood, shaking each man's hand. It was time for him to get back into the ER for the next patient.

"Thank you, Dr. Timms." Both men spoke as one as they rose with the doctor. As they moved to the elevator, both knew they had to get her this operation, no matter the cost. What was this all going to involve? Dr. Roberts would fill them in on the whole picture, wouldn't he?

As they reached the floor, Rhys held his breath. It was time to go and find her room. Nearing Skylar's room, both men were unsure of themselves. They stood and sat at intervals; they had been there four hours when the Blackwells arrived.

Rhys decided he wouldn't move from her side; he would be there when she woke.

Rhys stood and shook hands with Harry. "Hi, she, I don't even know what to say."

Jean was crying, needing to reassure herself Skylar was okay. Going over to the bed, she leaned down and kissed her forehead. "I love you baby girl."

Skylar thought she could hear Rhys, but he sounded very far away. Why didn't they leave her alone? It was peaceful here, wherever here was. She wanted to enjoy these feelings going through her.

No, there's his voice again. Was he to haunt her even here? What was he saying? Skylar was straining to hear, but to no avail. The words were fading in and out, and she only caught bits and pieces of what was said.

Rhys was saying anything he could think of.

"Sweetheart, don't leave me."

"I'm here with your father."

"Harry and Jean are here, too."

"Dammit, I won't let you do this to us."

"You get this through your head –"

"Get your ass back to the present and us!"

"Damn!" Why wasn't there any change? Could she hear what he was saying?

"Skylar, I love you more than life itself."

"If you leave me, I doubt I'll be able to go on without you." Rhys dropped his head with tears running down his face.

"How are we to get married, if you continue to lay there and sleep our life away?"

Skylar heard more and more of what was being said. It had to be a dream.

"Skylar, I'm praying you can hear. Please don't let John win in the end. Let the two of us be the winners." Rhys felt he was losing the battle of his life. Bowing his head, he began to pray again. If God would let her live, if it came down to letting he go in the end … no, he didn't think he could do that.

Jean and Harry were standing with him, rubbing his shoulders. "Son, our girl is strong. We need to believe she is going to pull through."

"Now Skylar, what is this foolishness of scaring the parents of your heart this way?" Even Harry broke down at this point, though he was trying to be strong.

Just as Rhys was going to rise, he saw movement in Skylar's face. It looked like she was going to open her eyes. He watched with anticipation, urging her on. "Come on baby."

There it was, a small blink of her eyes. Now he had to get her awake and get her consent for the operation to save her life.

Matt reached for the call button.

The nurse walked in and looked at Skylar. "I believe this little lady will be waking shortly."

"How soon?" Rhys questioned her.

"Sir, it will probably be a day or a little more before she is fully coherent. She will be in and out, each time it will get longer as she progresses."

Rhys wanted her awake now. "They need the decision about the operation now."

"Listen, why don't the four of you take a break and go get some coffee, maybe a bite to eat? Or just go for a walk. We can clean her up and get her changed," the shift nurse said.

"Son, let them do their job. Let's step out and the four of us go for a walk," Matt said.

Rhys had had enough. "Listen, old man."

Jean spoke up. "Rhys, I know she wouldn't want this, let's grab a bite to eat like the nurse said. We won't be far."

"Rhys, think of Skylar right now, not the other stuff," Harry added.

Sighing, Rhys knew they were right. Nodding, he let them lead him out of the room to the elevators. Rhys looked unshaven, black circles were under his eyes, and he was a total grouch. "I'm sorry, I want her back so bad."

"We all do," Jean said as she hugged him.

Lack of sleep and frustration was taking its toll on them. They walked the halls in the hours to come, taking turns waiting for her to come around. A doctor approached them after talking at the nurse's station.

"I take it you are with Skylar?" he asked, extending his hand to each one of them. "I'm Dr. Roberts. Sorry I had a couple of emergencies to deal with, but I have kept in touch with the nursing staff. I assume you've been waiting awhile."

"You're damn right, and you took your own sweet time getting here," Rhys stormed at him.

"Rhys, really." Matt said with exasperation.

"Rhys, he just said there had been some emergencies." Jean took his hand.

"I'm sorry, it's hard waiting and not being able to do anything for her." Rhys felt like shit for taking this out on the doctor who was doing the most to help.

Dr. Roberts understood how they all felt. He would be feeling the same if he was in their shoes. "It's alright. Like I said before, I've been in constant contact. And Dr. Timms was here if they would have needed him. Not much can be done until she wakes up. If you all would take a seat, I can be frank." Dr. Roberts said.

"Skylar might —" Rhys started, but the doctor held his hand up for him to stop.

"It will be awhile yet till she knows where she is, let alone if anyone is with her. Now, let's get started?" At their nod, he began explaining about the tests and what was shown. Then they talked about what needed to be done. He did keep a few things back because he needed to tell Skylar before anyone else.

★★★

By the next afternoon, Skylar opened her eyes, blinking at the light. The light hurt her eyes. She wanted to go back to sleep, where it was peaceful.

"Skylar, don't you dare go back away from us. We haven't had you fighting for nothing. Do you hear me? I won't have it. Dammit, I need you to make my life right again." Rhys said with emotion, while tears were running down his cheeks.

"Thir – thirsty!" It was so hard to talk with this dry throat.

"Sweetheart, I'll give you all the water you want. Just stay awake. Hearing your voice after so long is an answer to all of the prayers we've been saying." Rhys buzzed the nurse.

It was as though Skylar improved by the hour. She was able to stay awake longer than the staff had thought. By the next morning, Rhys knew the time was approaching to bring up the subject of the operation Dr. Roberts had talked about. So with the support of all, it was decided they would try and talk with her in the afternoon.

"Skylar, now you're staying awake, it's time to talk about a few things," Jean said while holding her hand.

Rhys felt she needed to know what he felt. "Skylar, I love you more than you could know. Can you listen to us?"

"Rhys, I –" Skylar was afraid of what was going to be said.

"No, let me finish. I've talked to Dr. Roberts, and I know about the problems. He said you have to have this operation as soon as possible." Rhys tried to speak gently.

"No!" Skylar got out.

"What do you mean, no? Dammit Skylar, I don't want to find you only to lose you again. You are my life," Rhys said with emotion.

"Rhys, I don't want to endanger our baby." Skylar had tears in her eyes.

"Don't be stupid. You're having the operation and it's final," Rhys said sternly.

"It's not up to you. Now, drop it." Skylar was getting upset, didn't he care?

"I would if I could. I want you alive more than anything else in this world. Is it so wrong of me to want that?" Rhys was trying to hold his anger in.

"No, but –" Skylar was unsure of what to say to this.

"No. You're going to listen to me. I never got to interrupt you, you wrote a letter. Well, sweetheart, you and I are going to do this face to face. So you listen, and listen well.

"If the baby would happen to die, sure I'll grieve for it. But only because it's a part of both of us. If you die, I not only lose a child by us, but you as well. Then there is no chance at another child of ours. The doctor assured me there can be other children."

"Rhys, please, you don't understand," Skylar said quietly, with tears running down her face.

"No, you're the one who doesn't understand. You may very well die tomorrow, next week, or even a month from now. Then what? Your refusing the operation will have been for nothing in the end.

"Answer me this, what will be left? No, I'll answer it. Nothing, not you, or the baby. I'll have neither. What will be left of our love, but memories? As nice as it would be, they won't get me through the rest of my life.

"You know as well as I do you're not far enough along to save the baby one way or another." Rhys took a deep breath.

"Rhys, I can't take this." Skylar was crying.

"You may think of me as a monster, but I'm not. I won't let you kill yourself." Rhys didn't know what else he could do.

Skylar looked at this man she loved as Jean stepped forward. "Rhys, I understand where Skylar is. I lost three babies. As much as I love Skylar, I still grieve for those little ones to this day. Have you not been grieving for the child you lost, even though it has been gone over five years?"

Rhys rubbed his hands over his face. What was he to do?

"Rhys, I can't bring myself to do anything which will hurt our child. John caused me so much pain, but it would be nothing compared to letting our child go. I don't know if I could live with myself after." Skylar broke down, not able to finish her thoughts.

Rhys opened his mouth to speak, just as the nurse came in. "Mr. Cantrell, I think you all had better leave now. Skylar needs rest, not this arguing."

"Don't you tell me to leave!" Rhys ranted.

"Either you leave on your own, or I'll be forced to call security and have you forcefully removed," the nurse said in a calm, authoritive voice Rhys was beginning to hate.

"Listen —" Rhys began when Jean and Harry touched his arms.

"No, you will listen to me. I'm the nurse in charge and you are causing my patient more harm than good. So if I'm forced in the direction I've said…Well, then it happens you will be banned from this hospital until further notice. Do you understand?"

"Rhys, let's go for a walk son. This isn't helping things." Harry tried gently to pull Rhys away from the nurse.

"Fine, I'll go for now. I will be back tomorrow, you can count on it."

"Thank you for at least going today. I am serious, the patient needs her rest, not these upsets you seem to be causing." the nurse stated.

Rhys turned and quit the room.

Jean went over and hugged Skylar. "We'll see you later, dear. He can only think of you, he doesn't see anything else right now. When men are afraid, they are one dimensional in their thinking. I love you, my daughter."

"Love you too." Skylar said with a sob.

The three men were waiting for Jean in the hallway.

Rhys spoke first. "We must speak with the doctor, see if there is some other way around this. See if there are any other treatments she can have."

Matt didn't know what to think; he had never felt this numb.

Rhys though there had to be another way to get Skylar into the operating room without her consent.

CHAPTER 29

RHYS DIDN'T GO BACK TO the rental with the others. He needed a drink and to be by himself. The drinking wasn't helping, but maybe walking would. He called Harry to tell him he was walking to clear his head, and not to wait up for him to get back.

To operate they needed consent.

Rhys went over everything they had learned. The bottom line was that something had to be done. If they were married, could he make the decision if it came down to it? If she took a turn for the worse in the weeks to come, could he, as her husband, make the decisions for her? Pushing his hand through his hair, he just didn't know now. Thinking over all that Jean and Skylar said added a different slant on the picture.

Rhys watched the sun come up over the ocean, then headed back to the house to get a couple hours of sleep.

In the afternoon, Rhys returned to the hospital in a sour mood. Walking into the room, he paused to see how she looked. "How are you today?"

Skylar looked up. "A little better, I think."

Taking a deep breath, while running his hand through his hair, Rhys spoke. "I think we should get married."

Skylar was startled. That was not what she was expecting. "That was such a well-thought and loving proposal. Now I wonder why I would ever want to refuse it."

"Dammit, Bree —" But before Rhys could get any more out of his mouth Skylar immediately rounded on him.

"You stop right there. I'm Skylar Evans, not your damn wife, Bree. For the last time, I'm telling you I'm Skylar, not her anymore. I really am Skylar." She collapsed back on her bed, racked with sobs.

Rhys was angry, not only with himself, but with Skylar for even thinking he had meant to call her Bree. He had been about to point out she died with their child, but he didn't want to lose it all again.

It so happened the doctor was outside the room. Upon hearing what was going on, he entered. Looking from one person to the other, he pointed to Rhys and spoke in a no nonsense voice. "Out, right now. I'll have no more of this. Do you understand me, Mr. Cantrell? You wait for me in the hall, I want to talk to you. Right now, I've got to get Ms. Evans settled."

Rhys stood there, staring at the man. Dr. Roberts cleared his throat before he spoke again. "Evidently, you didn't hear me the first time. I said leave. And I mean now."

Rhys turned and went into the hall to pace while waiting on the doctor. Matt, Jean, and Harry arrived at the same time the doctor was coming out of Skylar's room.

Rhys went to speak and Dr. Roberts said, "Not here. In my office."

They followed the doctor down the hallway. "Take a seat, everyone. I'll give it to you straight. These arguments aren't doing her a bit of good. It's doing a great deal of harm. She doesn't have the strength at the moment to handle this. I'm asking you not to see her for the rest of the day. And she has asked for all of you to be banned admittance to her room."

Jean's sharp breath was audible to the others. "All of us?"

"Dammit Rhys," Harry and Matt both said.

Dr. Roberts looked from one to the others. "Right now, I happen to agree with her. Each of you have your emotions flying every which way. That isn't helping her."

Rhys leapt to his feet. "What the hell do you mean, she refuses to see me?"

Dr. Roberts raised his eyes. "This is a prime example of what I've been telling you."

"Sit down Rhys." Matt had grabbed his arm. "We need to listen and do what is best for her health."

Rhys complied, but wasn't about to listen to excuses. He himself was about to the end of his own rope.

"All I'm asking is for you to give her a day of calm and peace before seeing her again. After, we'll go in and talk to her. But I'm warning you, you better remain calm. She won't have the operation, so you all need to be prepared if she would fall into a coma or if the worst would happen. You need to get things settled once and for all." Dr. Roberts wanted the seriousness of the situation to sink in.

"I have other patients to see now, so I have to go. Think over what I've said carefully," he added as he stood to shake hands with all.

They departed the hospital with much on their minds.

Over the next day, each of them talked about how they felt.

Rhys had to make plans as to how to get Skylar to marry him, so if something happened, at least she was his wife for a time. He had prayed and prayed to find the answers. Nothing felt right in the end. What was in her best interest was the question.

Dr. Roberts talked things over with Skylar again. "You need to understand how dangerous your condition is, first and foremost. It is life-threatening to you and your children. Yes, I said children. We saw three on the last sonogram. If your uterus tears more, it will cause severe bleeding and the babies can suffocate. You need to decide if you want to talk this over with the father, before it's too late. It is in the best interest of you and your children."

Skylar was shocked by what he was telling her. "Please don't tell I'm having more than one baby."

The next morning, Dr. Roberts and Rhys went towards Skylar's room. Just outside, he stopped them before going in. "Remember my warning about upsetting her."

Rhys nodded. "I remember."

Rhys walked over to the bed and spoke hesitantly. "Skylar, can we talk?"

"I – I guess so." she said, knowing she was resigned to her fate.

"What I'm about to say, may well upset you. It isn't my intent, believe me. But it needs to be said. Okay?" Rhys had not felt this unsure in a long time.

"Fine." She wasn't going to make it easy.

"Please don't say anything till I'm finished. In case I have to back up over something coming out wrong. I don't want to argue.

"First, I don't want our baby born a bastard." This made Skylar flinch. "I know how you felt finding out about your parents. I don't think you want that for our child. If you make it through this, and have the child, then that's all fine and good, but what if you would happen to die?" Rhys swallowed audibly, but continued.

"Marry me, and give our child my name. Don't cheat our baby."

Skylar felt hopeless. What else could she do? "Yes, I'll marry you."

"Grandfather has a friend who is a judge. He could cut out the red tape. If you wouldn't mind getting married here, we might be able to be married by tomorrow," Rhys continued.

With no emotion in her voice, Skylar answered. "I guess."

They were married at ten o'clock in the morning, the very next day.

Skylar became critical shortly after. This gave Rhys the responsibility of deciding what would be the best for all concerned.

There was no choice. Rhys told them to maintain her pregnancy, and operate. If the baby was meant to live, then it would be God's will. He wouldn't deny Skylar's wishes. But, he did say that if Skylar's life was in danger at any time, they were to save her at all costs. He couldn't lose her. He signed all the necessary forms.

Jean and Harry approached Rhys as he was sitting in the hospital chapel. "Son, we are right proud of you, following her wishes. Well done. I think you might be a keeper."

Three hours later, they took Skylar to intensive care. Rhys stood and watched as the doors shut once again.

The doctor came up behind Rhys, then cleared his throat. "Mr. Cantrell, Rhys?"

At this, Rhys whipped around. "How did it go?"

Dr. Roberts was smiling. "It was a success for all. We wait and watch now. And praying won't go amiss."

Skylar began coming out of the drugs from surgery a little later, but things were fuzzy.

She was pissed. How could Rhys have endangered their child? Dammit, she didn't agree to the operation. Did their child mean so little to him?

They came to take Skylar down for a couple of tests. They were unsure about something to do with her pregnancy, and they didn't think she would be able to carry the babies full-term unless she was on complete bed rest. She had to stay calm and collected, too.

Rhys let her rant at him all she wanted and never raised his voice to her. If she hated him, he would live with it as long as she was alive. He hired a full-time nurse to stay at the house with them.

As the weeks went by, Skylar began getting depressed. She wasn't allowed to do anything, and Rhys wouldn't even argue with her. She missed the fire they created. Rhys treated her with kid gloves ever since they had returned home.

She was six months along now, and her last appointment they had done a new sonogram. The results were eye opening. Skylar wouldn't let Rhys go in with her during any appointments. Skylar had asked the Doctor if they could make love since she had come so far with her health. The doctor said, as she had healed so well, he saw no reason they couldn't as long as they were careful. He also told them they didn't need the nurse with them any longer. They were even allowed to return to Pennsylvania.

All the rest had done its job.

Rhys flinched when she told him they could have relations. *Was everything he was doing just for their baby? Did he still think of Bree and their child?* Now Skylar was jealous of her dead sister.

Jean came to stay and go to the rest of Skylar's appointments with her since she wouldn't let Rhys in with her. When she found Skylar crying, she asked, "Skylar, you must stop this. You have been doing so well with taking care, what has happened? You're going to make yourself ill, then it will affect the baby also."

"And what do you know or understand? I'm married to a man because of the children I'm carrying, and the person I look like."

Jean was taken aback. "Now you listen to me young lady. After everything the two of you have been through, you can't think this way. And did you say children?"

"It's true! When was the last time Rhys really kissed me, let alone show his feelings in any way?" Skylar shook with anger.

"Young lady you let me tell you something. That man sat in the chapel praying for direction, then he told them to follow what you wanted. And at the last moment he stopped the doctor while he was going into the operating room and told them to save you above anything. Even now, I think he is unsure of you. He is afraid you will want to leave. Maybe if you would quit feeling sorry for yourself, you might just see how much he loves you. And by the way, I'll ask again, did you say children?"

Skylar asked through her tears. "Are you sure about this?"

Jean looked at her. "Yes, I am."

"Yes, I said children, but I want to keep it to myself for now, please."

Jean was shaking her head. "You are going to keep him on his toes for the rest of his life, aren't you girl?"

Skylar was sobbing now for a different reason. It was time to get her spirit back. She sent for Rhys, and would take no excuses. They were going to talk. Once and for all, she wanted to hear the truth. Did they have a future together?

Rhys didn't know what to think when Skylar had said she wanted to talk. What did it mean? Did she want to stay and make things work, or did she want her freedom? If it was the latter, he doubted he could give it to her. If she left, it would kill him. He had never been so frightened by what he might hear her say.

It was better to get it over with, so up to their room he went. Knocking on the door frame, he went into the room and spoke as fast as he could.

"You sent for me." Rhys asked in a toneless voice.

With a quiver in her own voice, Skylar began. "I have many things I need answers for. Will you give me those answers?"

"How can I not answer your questions? You have every right to know what's been happening," Rhys ended on a sigh.

"It's just, damn, I don't even know where I want to begin," Skylar stammered.

Rhys's nerves were about to burst. "Dammit, Skylar, just say what in the hell's on your mind. Either you want to know or you don't. Or is it you want to say things, not ask?"

Skylar wasn't sure where to start. "Rhys, please! We haven't actually been talking up a storm lately, now have we?"

Closing his eyes, Rhys felt like shit. "I guess not. I'm sorry."

"I'm sorry, too." Skylar said weakly.

They sat looking at each other. Neither wanted this to end in a shouting match.

"Rhys, did you really tell them to save me above all else? And why?" Skylar wanted to know, but was afraid at the same time.

"Skylar, lets backtrack first, before I answer. When I'm finished maybe most of your questions will be answered without even having to ask. Please, let me say it without you getting angry and only hearing half of what I do say.

"First and foremost, I love you as I love no other person. You will always come first in my life. You are more precious than life itself to me. You've misunderstood so much of what was happening. I know some of it was my fault, because of shutting you out. It wasn't done intentionally to hurt you. I was dealing with things on my own for years. I didn't stop to think maybe you could've helped me. So I hurt you without meaning to.

"What you overheard, the day you came home from the hospital, was me being eaten up by guilt, over the past and the present. I kept overlaying you on top of Bree, thinking you both could have been in that hole. And it was killing me more about you, so I felt guilt for that also."

Skylar was about to speak, but Rhys held up his hand. "Let me finish, before I can't."

"The guilt was because not one, but two lives, were lost, then almost two more. I hated Bree for leaving, and I carried that hatred around for so long before I found it was for nothing. Maybe a part of me did love her, I don't really know. I do know we would have never lasted.

"You have to know what I feel for you is so much more. It takes in my whole person. In your letter, you left me to cherish your heart, well I do. You were wrong about the small part of mine, because you already had the whole thing. It was yours for the taking, I think, from the beginning."

With tears in her eyes, and voice quivering, Skylar spoke. "Oh Rhys."

Rhys continued. "The day in the hospital, when you thought I was calling you Bree —" Seeing her stiffen at this, he hurried to continue.

"I wasn't really. It was just you were acting like her then, and I was going to tell you about it."

"Do you really mean all this?" She asked.

"More than anything else in this world. Skylar, you have the power to cut me off at the knees with no more than a look. I'm nothing without you. You are truly my other half, believe me."

"Oh Rhys, I want to," Skylar said with tears running down her face.

"Then believe with your heart baby, not your mind." Rhys had a smile on his face.

"I've been scared. I didn't think it was possible that it was me you loved. And here I've been fighting with you tooth and nail. Why have I been so stubborn and foolish? Can you forgive me for the things that happened?"

Shaking his head, no, with the biggest grin, he said, "There is nothing to forgive. We both made mistakes. I love all of you, as I hope you love me."

Skylar was grinning back. "Yes, Rhys, I do love you."

"I wouldn't want you any other way. You keep me on my toes and talk back." Leaning down close to Skylar, he looked right into her eyes and spoke in a very serious tone.

"But there is one thing. Do you think, maybe we could kind of kiss and make up now?" Rhys said with the grin he was known for reaching his eyes.

"Oh you, come here before I decide to bop you instead. I love you so much Rhys."

"And I love you." Rhys enfolded Skylar in the most loving embrace they had ever shared. Then they sealed their love with a kiss, which should remain behind closed doors.

Epilogue

The Cantrell family was going to the ranch to spend time with Paul. The episode with John all those months ago had taken its toll on him. There were still many things coming out as to why it happened. They were all healing, trying to put it in the past.

Brandon had told them they all were to take a break. The months since that time had been hectic with the business doubling. He had got Matt and the Blackwells to join him and all of his boys and their females on this trip. All of them in one place for a change.

As things returned to normal, Skylar adjusted quite easily. If being married to a Cantrell could ever be termed as normal. She still had three weeks until her due date. Jean was still the only one who knew about the extra surprise they were in for. She thought Chelsea might know she was going to have a multiple birth by her size, but hadn't asked.

Right now, they were all enjoying a plane ride to the ranch, eager to see Paul, Jordan, and even Sarah again.

We're having triplets, she thought with a grin. Seeing the grin, and watching Skylar rub her stomach, Jean knew what she was thinking. "You are going to cause havoc in this family, you know."

Skylar laughed out loud.

"What's so funny, sweetheart?" Rhys asked.

"I'll let you now one of these days real soon." Skylar smiled at him. She was looking forward to shocking the socks off all these Cantrells.

Nothing rattled these men, except babies, Chelsea had told her. Skylar liked Alan's wife. They had become close since things had settled down. Seeing the kids running around the plane gave her such joy.

Skylar felt cramped in her seat, and so she decided to stand and stretch, to go talk to the kids. Just as she rose, a small pain went through her. All she could think of was, *Rhys is going to kill me.*

"Rhys, could I lay down in the back till we land?" Skylar asked.

Rhys was worried. "Are you okay?"

"Just a little uncomfortable right now." Skylar looked at Jean.

They landed and there were enough cars to take them all up to the ranch as a single entourage. Upon reaching the house, they went to get out of the car, when a pain caught Skylar and caused her to double over. Rhys had been coming around the car and reached his wife before she touched the ground. As he was lifting her, he felt wetness. Skylar's water had broken.

"Dammit Skylar," he said.

"Not now, Rhys," Skylar said through clenched teeth.

"I told you we should have stayed home, close to the hospital."

Alan laughed because he knew how Rhys was feeling. "Better take her in and put her on the bed. It looks as though the newest member of our family is in a hurry to come into this world. Well, Chelsea, shall we go and see to what needs done?"

"Dammit, Skylar. You are not, I repeat, you are *not* springing this birth on us now. For heaven's sake, we just got off the plane." Rhys was getting worried.

"Rhys, I …think …I… might… be … giving … birth … now," she said through another contraction.

The four of them reached Rhys's room, and Alan sent Rhys back out. "We need to get her ready, just in case she does have the baby. It could be hours yet. Maybe call the hospital and tell them what is happening and to send an ambulance out here."

As Rhys turned to go, the doorway was filled with people. "Everyone needs to back up and sit down for awhile."

Ethan looked at Rhys as he passed. "Rhys."

"Not now." Rhys was on a mission to get the hospital ready and get the ambulance out here to the ranch ASAP.

When he came back down, Ethan grabbed Rhys by the arm. "Listen Rhys, this isn't going to happen now, is it?"

"I guess, I don't know." Rhys wasn't sure.

Harry looked at Rhys and laughed. "Son you better sit down before you fall down. Damn, you look as though you're in worse shape than Skylar is."

Craig and Matt were laughing to themselves.

Ethan looked almost as white as Rhys did. "I wish the two of you would quit having all this drama. It's been going on since you met."

Craig couldn't hold the laughter back. "You guys are scaring all the single ladies here. Our girlfriends are shocked. Do you know if this will be a new family tradition?'

Brandon shook his head. "All of you know this is something which will happen often, if you fall in love."

Motioning to the livingroom, where the girls were keeping the children entertained, Craig added, "How do you expect we'll ever get them to come with us again?"

Rhys turned and glared at his cousin, then his brother. "Dammit! What the hell do either of you know? She could very well die."

Craig spoke up. "Rhys, you know the doctor released her as fully recovered last month. He said there were no more problems. Do you think she would want you carrying on like this? You know what she would say. Women have babies every day in this world."

"I know," Rhys said, resigned to the life he chose, with a glad heart.

Alan came out, and yelled down the stairs. "Well, brother, there's no more waiting. Do you want to be part of the birth or not? If you do, you better follow me now."

Most of the people listening rose to follow along. Alan turned and raised his eyebrows at them. "I think the rest of you need to wait down here."

There were groans all around.

Rhys wasn't being left out of this for anything. As he got to Skylar's side, she yelled at him. "What kept you?"

"Sorry sweetheart," he answered with a smile.

"You almost missed everything," Skylar groaned.

"Never, baby. Never again," Rhys said with all the love he felt for this woman.

Skylar moaned. "Rhys, I need you. Hold my hand."

He did her bidding instantly. "It's alright baby." He was glad he was sitting. He didn't want to embarrass himself by falling over due to the excitement and the overwhelming tension in the room.

He heard Chelsea. "I do believe the little devil's coming."

After the first baby was out, within seconds, another was appearing. Rhys and Skylar looked on in wonder as the babies were being cleaned up. All of a sudden, another pain hit Skylar. Alan turned back to her, just as a third child was trying to enter the world.

Alan laughed then. "So dear, sweet Skylar, you were holding out on the family. Are you trying to continue the Cantrell line all on your own?"

Rhys looked first at his wife, then his three children. He was speechless.

"Let's see, Rhys, you haven't said a word yet. A big accomplishment on your little wife's part. I would say a major feat because she caused your complete silence. Of course it did help, your children being born."

"Is that all? There aren't any more in there, are there?" Rhys asked, stunned beyond belief.

"No, I think she had all she's going to. You have two sons and a daughter to thank God for. They seem healthy, and will be checked out at the hospital when we get them transported." Alan could hear the siren of the ambulance in the distance. It was probably just now entering the gates of the ranch.

"You had better think up a few good names for them, though. There are a few men out there who are going to have to be distracted about not being allowed back here for the birth. After all, they planned on helping Skylar out with this. Or didn't you know. They need to have their hands in everything. You remember Dad when we were having ours?" Alan laughed at the last part he added.

"No, we didn't." Skylar and Rhys both answered.

Chelsea looked at her husband, tilting her head to the door. "Alan, stop the teasing. Skylar, you rest now. The two of you enjoy those babies for a bit. The ambulance should be here soon."

At the couple's nod, she motioned for Alan to leave and give the new family a few minutes alone.

While going out the door, Alan stopped and looked back. "I don't know why we have to leave, they didn't even know we were still in the room."

"Hush, remember when we had ours," Chelsea said with a smile, remembering the warm embraces and the pride glowing from Alan.

"Yes dear, I do." Alan was thinking the same thing as his wife.

★★★

"Well Mrs. Cantrell, I take it you knew we were having more than one child?" Rhys asked with a raised eyebrow.

"Rhys, I'm sorry, but you don't know how hard it was to keep quiet. You had worried so much that I knew if I told you, you would try to smother me. As it was, I was very rarely out of your sight anyway," Skylar said on a sigh of joy.

"I guess I would have. I love you Skylar Cantrell."

"I love you, Rhys."

The ambulance arrived and they loaded everyone up to be transported. By the time they reached the hospital, they were sure what they wanted to name their children.

"Well, what should we name our children sweetheart?" He asked with a smile.

Rhys Alan.

Brandon Paul.

Reagan Joy.

If they thought things were going to be calm now, they were in for a big surprise. They would have to wait and see what these three Musketeers would get up to.

THE END

Printed in the United States
By Bookmasters